EH 3/09

VW
5/17

LADIGAN

A mysterious telegram summons manhunter John Ladigan to the Colorado town of Timmervale, which is locked in the iron grip of the powerful and vicious Timm family. Ladigan finds himself confronted with a decision to make, the outcome of which well may leave a young woman in the clutches of a sadistic madman. Add to that a series of brutal murders and the disappearance of his closest kin and the manhunter winds up snared in a mystery far bigger than he ever imagined. Can Ladigan overcome the demons of his past and present before he too, vanishes into thin air?

D1415961

For Tannenbaum. Missed always.

after he'd jammed his lips over hers, a taste that reminded her of cold bacon grease gone rancid. A taste that now mixed with the gunmetal flavor of her own blood from a gash inside her cheek. The stench of his sweat blended with horse leather – fine horse leather if she knew the Timms – and gin; the aroma of her own perfume, applied heavy enough to cover the stink of sin. Other things, in glimpses: red *fleur de lis* wallpaper flashing, buttery lanternlight streaking, punctuated by sparkling variegated stars exploding across her vision after the blackness vanished.

She hit the floor hard, but couldn't have said it caused any pain. Likely being halfconscious saved her from further damage, though it snapped her senses clear, a favor for which Prilla didn't know whether to thank her Lord Almighty or curse the hell out of him.

She pushed herself up into a half-sitting, half-twisted position, sweeping the tight ringlets of her strawberry-blonde hair away from her face, then tenderly kneaded her jaw where his fist had struck. *Now* she felt pain, biting singing shards of it.

'Hell, you should have been nicer to me, Prilla.' The words came with a sarcastic repri-

6

LADIGAN

by

Lance Howard

Dales Large Print Books
Long Preston, North Yorkshire,
BD23 4ND, England.

British Library Cataloguing in Publication Data.

Howard, Lance
    Ladigan.

    A catalogue record of this book is
    available from the British Library

    ISBN   1-84262-439-3 pbk

First published in Great Britain 2005 by Robert Hale Limited

Copyright © Howard Hopkins 2005

Cover illustration © Longarron by arrangement with
Norma Editorial S.A.

Published in Large Print 2006 by arrangement with
Robert Hale Ltd.

Dales Large Print is an imprint of Library Magna Books Ltd.

Printed and bound in Great Britain by
T.J. (International) Ltd., Cornwall, PL28 8RW

CHAPTER ONE

She never saw the fist coming. One minute she peered into his cold gray eyes with a look of spite and defiance; the next her feet left the dust- and grime-coated floorboards. She sailed backwards, head over heels, across the mouse-gnawed, sheetless mattress.

No pain, not really. At least not at the moment of impact. Just a cracking sound that might have been her jawbone fracturing, though Prilla doubted that to be the case. She'd been hit harder, by stronger men than Jack Timm.

More likely the sound came from the snap of lightning in her head and flashing blackness that told her she had probably lost consciousness for just an instant, maybe two.

Damn peculiar, she reckoned, the things a body grew conscious of in those split seconds following a blow. As if time slowed to let her reflect on sordid details she had pushed to the back of her mind just so she could get through another hour with yet another man, the third tonight: the taste of his sour saliva mand, then a laugh that said it didn't matter whether she had done what he asked of her, an act not fit for even a lowly beast. Jack Timm enjoyed hitting women, wallowed in the feeling of power it afforded him and that was what he fancied more than a whore's favors. Jack Timm lusted for control, craved it like a drunkard gulping at the last drops from an empty gin bottle. Perhaps all men did, but Jack Timm took the breed to the extreme.

'You keep the hell away from me!' She spat the words, along with a stream of blood, trembling voice betraying the terror twisting at her innards. She dragged the back of her hand across her mouth, wiping away a dribble of scarlet. Realizing her peek-a-boo blouse had ridden down, exposing her left breast, she jerked her top back up, somehow feeling filthier in that moment than twelve years of whoring in saloons across Colorada Territory had ever made her feel.

Something in the depraved way he stared at her told her he would not stop with a mere beating, that he would never stop until she gave him the awful thing he had come for. Nobody in Timmervale refused a Timm, especially not a woman who sold her pleasures for a dollar a turn.

Prilla struggled to get to her feet, her ragged skirt getting twisted up in her legs, almost sending her back to the floor. Her legs quaked, and her heart threatened to pound its way clear out of her chest.

Jack Timm ran a hand over his wavy brown hair, smoothing it, then tugged down his brocade vest.

'You don't rightly expect I'll just let you walk on out of here and go back to business as usual, do you, Prilla?' The depraved look in his cold gray eyes strengthened. ''Less you've decided to accommodate me?'

'You go to hell!' She spat, blood and saliva, but it fell short of hitting him. Fury narrowed his eyes. He made a move to step around the bed, his intent clear. She lunged for the door, grabbing at the glass handle.

He moved faster than she expected. His arms vised around her belly, wrenching her away from the door. She twisted in his grip, unable to free herself. His leering face pressed closer to her, the sour bacon-fat odor of his breath assailing her nostrils.

'You're gonna do what I tell you, Prilla. You're gonna do it and you're gonna like it. Then we'll go back to how things was.'

Terror galvanized her into struggling like a cornered wolverine. His grip tightened, fingers gouging into the small of her back, as he tried to pull her towards the bed. She pounded at him with her fists, screamed out, knowing full well it would not do a damn bit of good. Not in this saloon. Not in this town.

In desperation, she let herself go limp. He must have reckoned she intended to comply, because for just an instant his grip slackened and an oily smile slipped across his thin lips.

The smile vanished like Plains fog under a scalding brass sun. She hoisted her knee, planting it squarely in his southern parts. Shock flashed across his narrow face, then purple stained his cheeks and gagging sounds sputtered from his mouth.

She jerked free and half-lunged, half-stumbled towards the door. Grasping the knob, palms slick with sweat, she yanked the door open and plunged out into the hallway. Flickering kerosene wall lanterns might well have been heavenly angels beckoning her into their arms.

A surging sense of relief washed through her. She'd escaped him, though she knew she would never again be welcome or safe in this no-good excuse for a town, but that didn't matter. All that mattered was she had gotten free without corrupting herself any more than years of selling her secrets already had.

Her elation was short-lived. She'd nearly reached the stairs leading to the saloon proper below when his hands grasped at her waist.

She tried to jerk away, only succeeded in twisting herself around to see his vile features profaned with hate, eyes glittering with the promise of revenge. Spittle flecked his lips. He was half-doubled, babbling noises like a branded calf, noises mixed with cussing and invective pledging she would damn well regret what she'd done.

In an effort to free herself, she pistoned out both arms and slammed her palms against his chest. The move snapped his hold and broke her free. He collapsed to his knees, still not fully recovered from her knee to his groin, but it mattered little, because momentum took her backwards a step too far. One moment her feet were on the edge of the stairway and the next they were kicking at empty air. Her arms came up in windmilling fashion and she twisted, but couldn't stop her plunge.

She hit three steps down and kept going. Repelling from the stair wall slowed her fall only a little. It wasn't a long flight, though she swore it sure as hell felt like it went on forever.

10

She came to rest at the bottom in a cloud of swirling sawdust. Hammering pain erupted from myriad points on her body, but miraculously she had failed to break her neck.

Around her patrons gaped and the tinkler piano went silent. Murmuring reached her ears. A sea of blurred faces swirled before her eyes. The faces focused and settled; she could see their vacant eyes and startled expressions. The other bargirls stared in shock.

'Help me, Clive...' The words came out strangled, barely coherent, as her gaze rose to meet the burly older man stepping from behind the polished bar flanking the right side of the room. His face was pinched, looking somehow demonic in the sallow light playing within the Durham haze clouding the room.

She blinked and Clive was a good five feet closer. Had she blacked out for an instant again?

'Can't he'p you, Prilla.' The older man shook his head. 'You's just a whore. Plenty more 'round here to take your place. You shoulda treated Mr Timm better.' The man glanced up the stairs and she turned her head, an act that sent slivers of pain through her skull.

Jack Timm was poised at the top of the

stairs, one hand braced on the rail, the other pressed against the wall. The look on his face promised the pain she'd experienced from the fall was a mere prelude to what she would receive once he made it down.

He took the first step, boot landing with the crash of a Winchester shot.

Her heart jumped and adrenaline surged into her veins. She struggled to push herself to her feet, modestly clutching her top higher for no reason she could have explained.

'Clive, please...' Her gaze locked with the barkeep's, blue eyes pleading.

'Sorry, Prilla.' A hint of sympathy in his tone, but no mercy. 'You know I can't. Mr Timm treats this town right good. Wouldn't be right to go against him.'

'Bastard!' She hissed the words through gritted teeth. 'You no-good lousy coward!' Anger helped dull the pain racking her body and she was able to grip the side of a table to pull herself completely up. Her legs wobbled, threatening to spill her, but determination born of terror held her upright.

Jack Timm had taken another three steps down, the oily grin back on his face. He knew he had her; he knew he had her because he owned this town and everyone in it, and even if she made it out the door not a goddamned one of the folks in this hell-hole would raise a hand to aid her.

She staggered for the batwings, stumbling into tables and rebounding, refusing to go down or give in. No one helped her, but no one stopped her, either. She reckoned she should be thankful for at least that much.

Cool night air splashed her face as she plunged outside. For the briefest of moments hope rose within her being. As quickly gone, replaced by the terror of hearing his boot-steps thundering across the barroom.

She forced herself into a clumsy trot, every inch of her body paining, jaw starting to swell and throb, heart thudding in her throat. Strangling pain gripped her chest, making her gasp. Fear propelled her onward, but it was no use; he would be on her in moments.

She stumbled off the boardwalk onto the dusty rutted street. She couldn't go on, couldn't breathe. Panic sapped the rest of her strength and will. Cascading pain and debilitating terror. Too much. Too much. She couldn't force herself to take another step.

She went down, hands thrust out before her, and slammed into the hard ground. A gritty medley of dust and manure assailed her nostrils, choking her. Her face collided with the dirt and she was tempted to just stay down, pretend she was dead, like someone had once told her to do with bears, but knew that would never work. Her labored breath and the clamor of her heart would give her away, and Jack Timm was more vicious than any bear could think of being.

Townsfolk gathered, some from the saloon, others coming from buildings, curious as to the ruckus. Shouts from Jack Timm, growing louder, like encroaching thunderclaps. A ring of people formed around her, as she tried to gain her feet again, only to fall back to her hands and knees. Her head rose, gaze lifting to settle on the bony form of Timmervale's town marshal.

'Hel ... help me, Pierson ... please...' Her words barely carried to the man.

The marshal, a vulture of a man with a protruding Adam's apple, shook his head, peering at her with a look of sympathy he quickly hid, as his gaze flicked across the street to the approaching form of Jack Timm.

'Prilla, what you gone and done?' Pity in his voice. Pity and the surety of St Peter telling her the gates to Heaven were closed and nothing she could ever say would open them.

'Timm ... he wanted...' She couldn't even say it.

'You shoulda given him whatever it was,

14

Prilla. You know that. You know anything the Timms want in this town they get.'

Tears glossed her eyes. 'Help me ... Pierson ... I done you special favors...'

He gave a slow shake of his head. 'Don't matter none now, Prilla. That's all in the past.'

She let out a strangled cry and a thought flashed into her head: this was what it was like to die for her sins. With the Devil in the form of a man descending upon her to commit unspeakable acts upon the shreds of her soul, with the smell of dung and brimstone in her nostrils and the taste of blood and vinegar on her lips. This was how it was to die for her sins. Too late to repent and too late to expect mercy.

She collapsed onto a hip and gazed upon her devil, who stopped before her. The spectators, her demons in waiting, had parted to let him through.

'Help me, please...' she pleaded one last time to the folks gathered around, hand reaching out, palm up.

'This here's a God-fearin' community,' said a woman wearing a yellow bonnet. 'You're a blight on the good name of this town.'

'This here's a Timm-fearin' community!' Prilla put all the spite into her voice she could muster, reckoning if she was going to Hell she was going kicking and screaming, damning the hypocrites of Timmervale to her last breath.

Jack Timm laughed, no humor in his tone. He squatted beside her, grabbing her chin between a thumb and forefinger, jerking her face towards him. She couldn't stop her lips from quivering.

'Nice speech, Prilla, darling, but the fine folks of Timmervale aren't listenin'. Fact, they aren't the only ones with listenin' problems, are they, now? You could have just done what I asked and made it so much easier on yourself.'

'What you asked ain't human.' She kept her voice defiant, determined to spite him to the last.

Oily grin, cold gray eyes mocking her.

'Now, see, that's what I mean. You still ain't listenin'. I just gave you another chance and you couldn't keep your filthy whorin' mouth shut.'

Jack Timm reached to his waist and drew a Bowie knife from the sheath at his belt. The blade caught the light from an outside hanging lantern and glinted cold stars across her face. Terror flooded her eyes and she tried to struggle but her strength was gone.

16

Switching his grip from her chin, he grabbed a handful of her strawberry-blonde hair and yanked her head up and back.

'Since your goddamn ears don't work I reckon you got no need of 'em.'

She knew his intent then, saw it reflected from his eyes like the glaring blackness of twin skulls. He wasn't going to kill her; no, that would be too easy, too fast, too leached of pleasure for a man like Jack Timm. He was going to maim her, ruin her for the little she was worth and leave her bleeding in the street. Maybe she would die then, maybe later. It wouldn't matter because dying would be welcome after days of bleeding and festering wounds.

'I-I'll ... tell...' she said, the sound strangled.

He yanked her head hard. 'No, you won't...' His oily smile widened and eager expectation danced in his gaze. Cold steel pressed against the crevice between the top of her ear and her head. Just a chill, no real pain, not at first. Then searing splinters of it, shrieking through her senses. A scream tore from her lips. Warm liquid flowed down both sides of her ear, as he sawed into the soft flesh, slowly, ever so slowly, like a master butcher carving the thinnest strips of meat from a butchered steer.

Her scream turned into pitiful mews and a number of the less hardy onlookers, mostly womenfolk, turned away. A look of pure disgust turned Marshal Pierson's features and he whirled and bent double, losing whatever it was he'd eaten for supper.

Gleeful laughter came from Jack Timm.

A gunshot stopped the sound. So abrupt, so unexpected, so startling, the entire crowd appeared to come off the ground in a collective jolt. The knife at her ear jerked away, the hand holding it yanking back. The Bowie landed in the dirt a few feet away. Jack Timm grabbed his knife-hand, blood trickling down his wrist. She clutched at her ear, her own blood running warm between her fingers.

The shock of the shot wearing off, the crowd's gaze focused on the source of the gunfire. Jack Timm's gaze jerked up as well, hate glittering in his cold gray eyes.

A peculiar numbness gripped her senses as her gaze settled on a man at the edge of the crowd, a man atop a big bay horse. In his hand, a Colt Peacemaker, white-gray smoke curling from its barrel, which was aimed dead center at Jack Timm's chest. A man whose face was handsome, yet battered by the elements, wearing a weatherbeaten Stetson, blue bib shirt, bandanna and worn trousers with a Bowie resting in his boot-sheath. Green eyes flicked to the marshal, but his gun stayed leveled on Timm. She reckoned if Timm made a move that would be the end of him. She prayed he would.

'Why didn't you stop this?' the rider asked Marshal Pierson, who wore the expression of a man just caught by his wife in a compromising position with another woman.

Pierson wiped a sleeve across his mouth.

'She's a whore. Mr Timm here's a respectable citizen.'

The man uttered a scoffing sound, gaze returning to Jack Timm, whose hate boiled in his eyes. She noticed the wound on his hand was little more than a scratch and that disappointed her.

'Respectable citizens in this town normally go 'round cuttin' off folks' ears?' He asked it of no one in particular and obviously wasn't expecting an answer. With his free hand, he reached to his neck and pulled loose his bandanna. He tossed it down to her and she caught it before it hit the dirt. 'Press that against your ear.'

She complied, blood quickly soaking the fabric, though the flow wasn't copious.

'Who the goddamn hell are you?' Jack Timm asked through clenched teeth. He plainly wanted to kill the man on the horse, but obviously knew he wouldn't make it more than a few inches before a bullet found him.

'Name's John Ladigan.' Little emotion punctuated the man's voice. The Peacemaker remained steady.

A look of – what? Recognition? Something. Something flashed across Jack Timm's face but vanished just as quickly.

'You know who the hell you're dealin' with, stranger?' Timm's words quivered with suppressed rage. Crimson flooded his face.

'A Mr Timm, I reckon.' John Ladigan's tone held an edge of mockery. 'Reckon you also figure you own this town. Given its name, you likely do. Must be a blood relation to Solomon Timm, if I figure right. Heard he had a no-good son.'

'Why, you–' Jack Timm made a move for his knife, but stopped in nearly the same movement.

'Go for your knife, Mr Timm.' Ladigan let something close to a smile drift over his lips. 'I'll pass along my condolences to your father when I tell him how you treat your women.'

Jack Timm glared, but made no further move towards his knife. Prilla wished the bastard hadn't left his gun belt hanging on the bedpost in the room above the saloon. Jack Timm was not normally a man to back down and had he been heeled he might have gone for his gun and got shot dead. She would have downright enjoyed that.

'You...' Ladigan ducked his chin towards her. 'Get up.'

She rose to her feet, legs shaking, holding the bandanna to her ear, the pain sharp and jabbing but tolerable. He beckoned her over and no one made a move to block her passage. She staggered against his bay, the scent of horse lather and leather heaven sent.

He switched the Peacemaker to his left hand and, leaning over, reached down. Eyes remaining steady on Jack Timm, he grasped her arm and hoisted her up behind him in the saddle. She instinctively clutched at his waist with one hand while keeping the bandanna pressed to her ear with the other.

John Ladigan shifted his gaze to the marshal.

'Where's the sawbones located?'

Pierson shifted feet, an uneasy expression tinting his face. Two other men in the crowd looked antsy suddenly, as if considering going for their guns. She knew they were employees of Timm, and her belly tightened with worry. What if both went for their weapons and killed her and the stranger?

'Ain't got one...' Pierson's voice broke slightly.

'Hell, you don't, you scrawny bastard!' She aimed all her spite at Pierson for not having the balls to stand up to Jack Timm.

'Tell me or I'll take off a piece of *his* ear with a bullet.' Ladigan nudged the Peacemaker at Timm and Pierson looked ready to soil his britches.

'Tell him...' ordered Jack Timm in a low voice that threatened to get even later.

'Down the street, three blocks, take a left.'

Ladigan offered a grim smile. 'Much obliged.' His gaze went back towards Timm, pausing at the two men at the edge of the crowd first. 'You got any notion of trying to stop me or followin', you best think real hard on it. Same goes for your men. I ain't in a particularly good temper after coming on somethin' like this.'

'Who the hell you think you are, Ladigan?' Timm stood from his squatting position, a measure of defiance coming over him.

'Just a concerned citizen...' He holstered his Peacemaker and gently heeled the bay into motion. She noticed he kept the corner of his gaze on Timm and the others, but no one made a move to stop them.

After traveling the three blocks, Ladigan steered the bay left into the side street and reined up in front of the doc's. A wooden sign swung from a pole embedded into the side of the shiplap building beside which ran an alley. Gilded letters on the sign read:

**Doc Porter's Medical Emporium
Eclectic Medicine Practitioner.**

The side walls of businesses stood opposite the sawbones' parlor.

'He ain't gonna treat me.' She stated it matter-of-factly. Her ear hurt like hell and every muscle quivered from residual fear.

'He'll treat you.' Ladigan stepped from the saddle and proffered a hand. Her feet hit the ground and he had to hold her up until she regained the strength to stand on her own. It took a few deep breaths and a measure of will power.

Her blue eyes settled on him with conviction.

'Not in this town. Timm owns it, owns the doc, too.'

'I gathered that from the way the crowd pitched in to help you back there. That's why I asked your marshal to tell me where the doc was located, 'stead of you. Figured it would put a bigger burr in Timm's saddle.'

'Ain't no joke, mister. He might kill you for helpin' me. No sawbones will risk Jack's temper, neither.'

'We'll see.' Ladigan's voice held no hint of fear. In fact, she heard a sort of lilt in it, as if he enjoyed taunting a man such as Jack Timm. She wondered what the hell was wrong with him. Didn't he know who Jack Timm was? Didn't everyone in these parts?

'It's only going to be worse when he catches up to us – and he will, that's for damn sure. He has a long memory – and a violent one.'

He smiled. Annoyingly. Taking her elbow, Ladigan guided her to the door and with a fist pounded on the panel. When no sound came from inside, he banged a second time. Stumbling footsteps came from within and the door opened. An older man with gray hair and mutton-chop side-whiskers peered out at them through bleary eyes.

'What do you want?' The man rubbed at his eyes.

'You Doc Porter?' asked Ladigan.

'Who's askin'?' The man was clearly irked at being interrupted from whatever he was doing. Prilla reckoned drinking, if the odor of gin coming from his breath were any indication.

'Name's Ladigan. This gal had her ear cut. She needs treatment.'

The doc's gaze shifted to Prilla. Disgust washed into his watery eyes.

'Ain't treatin' her, she's a whore, for chris'sakes.'

The Peacemaker appeared in Ladigan's hand as if by magic, leveled at Porter's stained white shirt.

'You'll treat her and you'll make it fast, *comprende?*'

Porter grumbled, eyes focused on the gun, then stepped back, grudgingly opening the door and motioning them in with a wave of his hand.

'What the Sam Hill happened anyway?' He led them through the front room, which was a waiting-area with stuffed sofas and comfortable chairs, into a small examination area adjoining. Firing up a couple lanterns, he beckoned Prilla to a chair. She didn't care for the way he staggered a bit and stank of booze, but her options weren't plentiful.

She sat and he pulled the bandanna away from her ear. The wound wasn't as bad as it had appeared for all the blood, but a good quarter inch was separated from her scalp.

Porter went to a cabinet that held various medicines – Dover's Powder, Hostetter's

Celebrated Stomach Bitters, Perund and Parker's Tonic – then brought back a handful of bottles, as well as a household needle and fiddle string, and set them on a small table next to the chair. He cleansed the wound with carbolic acid then applied powdered alum to constrict the small vessels. Prilla winced, as renewed pain singed her scalp. She glanced at the suturing material.

'I want laudanum.'

Porter blew out a disgusted sound.

'I ain't givin' a whore laudanum, for chris'sakes. Ain't treatin' you 'cause I want to, anyhow.'

'Give it to her.' Ladigan's tone brooked no argument.

Porter grumbled again, glanced at the Peacemaker now holstered at Ladigan's hip, went to a locked cabinet, and returned with a small brown bottle. He twisted off the cap and handed it to Prilla.

'S'pose she cain't pay, neither?' Porter shook his head.

Ladigan reached into his pocket and brought out a roll of greenbacks. He peeled off a number of bills and tossed them on the table.

'That'll cover it, plus, I reckon.'

Porter glanced at the cash, greed replacing

the disturbed look on his face.

'Reckon it will at that.'

Prilla sipped from the brown bottle as the sawbones threaded the needle and prepared to suture the wound.

'What the hell happened to her, anyhow?' Porter asked, hand starting towards her ear.

Ladigan frowned.

'Your Mr Timm gets a mite rough with his women.'

The doc's hand stopped midway, began to quake uncontrollably.

'Who'd you say?'

'Man named Timm.'

'I ain't working on this woman.' A gray color washed across Porter's face as the blood drained from his cheeks.

'You finish up.' Ladigan shifted his hand to his Colt, letting it rest atop the grip. 'I'm not a patient man, and I reckon Mr Timm won't waste a lot of time thinkin' up ways to get even with her.'

The doc shook his head.

'He won't want me treatin' her. He'll kill me for it maybe.'

Ladigan let a thin smile filter onto his lips.

'Maybe I'll kill you if you don't get on with it right quick.'

Porter glared, but his hand steadied as he

apparently judged Ladigan to be the more immediate threat. He began to sew the flesh together at the top of Prilla's ear. She winced with every puncture of the needle and it was all she could do not to curse at the top of her lungs. She took another drink of the laudanum, already feeling her head start to spin. She set the bottle on the table as he finished up and placed a small bandage to her ear.

Porter's expression turned grim, as he peered at Ladigan.

'Keep it clean. May fester, dependin' on how clean Timm's knife was.' He went to the cabinet again and brought back a small pouch. 'Brew this for her.' He tossed it to Ladigan, who tucked it in a pocket.

'What is it?'

'Willow-bark tea. Helps the pain, reduces fever if one occurs.' Porter plucked the laudanum from the table and returned it to the locked cabinet.

Ladigan helped Prilla from her chair. She staggered, legs wanting to go either way, some from the effects of her ordeal, some from the effects of the opiate. Ladigan guided her towards the door.

'Mister...' Porter said, and Ladigan turned his head to the doc. 'Don't come back. I won't treat her again, no matter what you threaten me with. If you know what's good for you you'll take her as far away as you can. Mexico, even. Timm ain't the type to forgive.'

'Obliged for the advice, Doc, but I got business round these parts. Mr Timm will just have to learn the meanin' of hospitality.'

'You're plumb lard-headed if you think that.' Porter's lips pinched into a grave expression.

'Ain't the first time someone's accused me of such.' Ladigan opened the door and stepped out into the night.

Jack Timm stood in the darkness of the alleyway next to the sawbones' office, two men from the crowd standing behind him. He watched as the man named Ladigan took the whore from the office and saw the bandage at her ear. So the sawbones had treated her, knowing full well what happened to anyone stupid enough to oppose the Timms. The old drunkard would pay for that.

Ladigan mounted and helped the girl up behind him, then started towards the main street. Timm watched him go, anger welling, though he restrained himself from interfering with their egress. Ladigan impressed him as a man not to be taken lightly. He would not be the easy mark the whores were.

Jack Timm had an idea who Ladigan was and why he was here. Although the man posed a potential danger, he doubted Ladigan knew much, otherwise all hell might have broken loose in the street. Yet it was no coincidence he was here.

What type of man was this Ladigan? Brave or simply loco?

Jack Timm was nothing if not a judge of character. He had to be because that judgement gave him control over others, and with that control, power. Defining a man's weaknesses was his specialty, but he needed more information on Ladigan.

'What do you want us to do, Jack?' one of the men, whose name was Burgis, whispered, nodding towards the departing riders.

An oily smile.

'Follow them. Beat the hell out of Ladigan and bring the girl back to me. We got unfinished business.'

The men nodded and skulked off, heading down the alley to horses they had tethered in back of the livery stable.

Anger boiled in Jack Timm's gut and sung in his veins. Ladigan had made a fool out of him in front of the entire town and that whore had gotten away scot free. He would show her what it meant to defy a Timm later. For now, he needed to pay a surprise visit to that no good sawbones and get his hand treated...

CHAPTER TWO

Ladigan made camp in a small clearing a half-mile outside of Timmervale, next to a stream that snaked its way through a woodland thick with blue spruce, cottonwood, aspen, fir and clustered brush. Tomorrow he'd see about securing a hotel in Timmervale, but at the moment he preferred to let the events of the evening settle down before risking another encounter with Jack Timm. Timm was likely half-drunk and when he sobered up things might be different. Ladigan hoped that would be the case, though the sawbones' anxiety and the marshal's lack of intervention gave him doubt.

Hell, what did it matter to him? The girl would likely head her own way with first light, and with her gone whatever Timm had been so fired up about might ride out with her, then Ladigan could get about his business.

You truly believe that, Ladigan? That Timm fella don't seem the type to forget a debt. And just where do you think that gal's gonna go without a horse, anyway?

He let out a sigh, not having thought that far ahead. He hadn't expected to ride into a situation his first night in town and wind up encumbered with a wounded whore. He'd figured on slipping in quietlike, then maybe heading on over to the saloon to feel out the barkeep, a breed who generally knew what was going on in a town, when and where. No suspicions raised, just a curious stranger making small talk. The girl had ruined that plan, made stealth impossible. The Timms knew he was here, and it wasn't a big step to figuring out why – if they had the hand in things Tom indicated in his telegram.

But what choice was there? He couldn't let Timm cut the woman's ear off.

Reining up, he dismounted, keeping his thoughts off his face. He offered her a hand down. She weaved some, likely from the effects of the laudanum more than her injuries. Guiding her to a deadfall, he lowered her to a sitting position, then attended to his horse. After tethering the bay to a cottonwood branch, he hauled his saddle to the deadfall, and tossed his bedroll beside it. The girl watched him, blue eyes cloudy, sort of vacant, and he decided it wasn't entirely the laudanum. Mild shock, he reckoned. Nearly getting an ear cut off and being hit – the swelling on her jaw and purpling bruise told the story – would do that to a body, even a hard woman such as a bar dove.

She wrapped her arms about herself and shivered. He unrolled the blanket and held it out to her. She looked at him as if waiting for him to demand some sort of payment for his generosity. He frowned, draped the blanket across her shoulders, then walked away.

The late-spring night air held a brisk bite, but it smelled oddly sweet. Somehow the serenity of the moonlight rippling within the stream water and the peaceful chirping of night creatures belied the seriousness of his mission and the situation he'd encountered in town, Just a month ago he might have relished camping under the stars on a case; he'd never cottoned to being confined for long, not since the days at the orphanage when a cramped dingy room served as his home. His and Tom's, two boys growing up with no mother or father. The open vastness of the land, the crisp air, the glassy singing of the stream: all calming such a short time back. Now ... not so much.

Tonight, they reminded him things weren't right, that something, some part of him, might be lost. A dark thought warned him that even if he discovered the answers he sought in Timmervale the old sense of freedom would never return. Things were different. Changed. Soiled.

He gathered an armload of tinder and dried branches, then piled them close to the girl. With a lucifer from his pocket, he got a fire started, coaxing it into a snapping blaze a short while later. She huddled closer to the flames, holding out her hands and letting the blanket fall back to her shoulders. She wasn't the prettiest woman he'd laid eyes on, yet fine enough, and it had been a spell since he'd known a gal in the Biblical sense. Strawberry-blonde ringlets covered the bandage, wisps of hair cork-screwing to either side of her face. Her nose might have been broken one time in the past, though it was small and not tilted enough to detract from her overall attractiveness. A smattering of freckles peppered that nose and her full lips invited soft whispers and unspoken pleasures. She had little bosom to speak of and was just a bit wide in the hips, but he could have fallen for a gal with her looks had he been another man and she another woman, one who wasn't bought for a few coins a night.

Hell, he couldn't think on that. He had a job to do, a mission. Going to his saddle-bags, which lay near the fire, he pulled out a blue-speckled enameled coffee-pot. After filling it with stream water, he fished the pouch of willow-bark tea from his pocket and set it to brewing. Returning to his bags, he located a tin cup.

'Hungry?' He didn't look at her directly, instead staring off towards the stream.

She muttered a soft 'no', and he nodded, but opened a can of beans for himself and devoured them cold. He couldn't recollect the last time he'd eaten, maybe yesterday, on the trail. He could go for days without food, subsisting on water from his canteen and burning will, but knew if he wanted to keep his strength up for what needed to be done he had to force himself to eat. Trouble was, he hadn't been able to stomach much beyond whiskey since the telegram came.

Going to the deadfall, he lowered himself onto it, a yard from the girl. He remained silent, in fact felt damned awkward sharing his campsite with a whore he didn't intend to bed.

'You're a damn fool for helpin' me, mister, you know that?' Her voice snapped him from his thoughts and rose a prickle of irritation.

'You're right welcome.' He made no attempt to hide the annoyance in his voice, though why he should give a damn was a question.

She glared, eyes washing clear, firelight sparkling within their emerald depths.

'No one in that town dares lift a finger against Jack Timm. What makes you different?'

'I'm not from these parts. Reckon I didn't know who he was at first.'

'You ain't heard of the Timms?' She looked skeptical, as if he had denied knowing Ulysses S. Grant was the President of the United States.

'I heard of 'em. Solomon Timm's one of the West's richest men, made a fortune with his gold and silver mines. They call him the Gild King of Colorado. Ain't likely anyone riding into Timmervale wouldn't make the association with its name. Didn't know him by sight, though. Son, neither. I assume Jack Timm is his son?'

She nodded, hate tightening her lips and narrowing her eyes.

'He is and he's a no-good sonofabitch.'

'He do that to you?' He ducked his chin at

36

her swollen jawline.

'He did, and more. He was about to kill me when you came up.'

'Ain't likely a man in his position would kill you in full view of witnesses.'

'You don't know him the way us whores do and in case you didn't notice, the townsfolk weren't exactly champin' at the bit to help me.'

'I noticed.'

'Number of gals gone belly-up after he was the last one to be with them. Knifed. He carries a knife.'

He shrugged. 'Doesn't prove anything. Every fella carries a knife and whores get themselves killed all the time.'

She bristled visibly at the remark and he cursed himself for being an insensitive bastard, but who the hell knew whores had feelings?

'The sonofabitch would have left me bleedin' in the street. I would have died just the same as if he'd shot me dead himself.'

'You're exaggerating.' He cast her a dubious look.

'Hell I am!' Her tone held genuine insult and he wondered why. Whores lied all the time or imagined things when hopped up on laudanum or belladonna. Why should she be peeled at him? Women were a damn mystery, whores in particular, way he figured it.

'He'll calm down once he sobers up.'

She laughed, and it annoyed him, though he couldn't have said why.

'He wasn't that drunk. He'll crawl out of wherever he spends the night tomorrow mornin' and be peeled as a sidewinder that got its tail stepped on. Jack Timm don't forget, he gets even. We best be far away from here soon, tonight even.'

'I ain't goin' nowhere. I got business in Timmervale.'

She looked at him as if he'd just told her he could lasso the moon.

'Are you plumb loco? Hell, I figured you must be, savin' a whore from Timm in the first place, but that damn well proves it. You go back to that town, he'll nail your hide to a wall.'

'I'll take my chances.'

'You're a fool, Ladigan.'

'Wouldn't be the first time someone accused me of such.'

She shook her head, then winced, pain pinching her face.

'Damn,' she said, gingerly touching her bandaged ear.

'What'd he want to go an' beat you for,

anyway?' he asked, before she could think of worse names to call him.

'He likes beatin' whores and he asked me to do something that ain't natural.' She shuddered.

'You refused?' He hoped that wasn't doubt in his voice, but it must have been because her glare got sharper.

''Course, I refused. You may not think much of my kind, but I got my limits.'

'Nice to hear that.'

She eyed him with a cocked eyebrow and a small measure of satisfaction at having gotten under her skin took him. Served her right for callin' him a fool.

'What's your name?' he asked her, reaching for the coffee-pot, then pouring the liquid into the tin cup and handing it to her. She blew on the tea and ghosts of steam whirled up in to the chilled air.

'Prilla, Prilla Barnes.'

Right pretty, he thought. He went silent as she sipped at the tea. After fifteen minutes passed she appeared to gain a measure of steadiness.

'What business you got in Timmervale that's so all-fired important you want to get yourself killed?'

'None of yours.' He had little desire to

explain his reasons to her. The annoyed look flashing onto her features gave him another tickle of satisfaction. Her type made an art form of persuading men to spill their secrets. She was used to getting what she wanted with her body and soft whispers. Had he been in a different frame of mind it might have worked, but not now, not when he had so much at stake.

'Hell of a way to make conversation.' She gulped the rest of her tea and tossed the cup to the sand with more force than necessary. 'Well, let's get this over with.'

She stood, letting the blanket fall away and for an instant she teetered, then regained her balance. Her fingers pried at the top of her skirt, starting it on a downward sway over her hips.

He jumped up and his Stetson tumbled from his head.

'What the hell you're think your doing?'

Confusion furrowed her brow.

'I can't be beholdin' to no man. Only way I got to pay you back.'

'Ain't necessary.' He couldn't tell whether she appeared more shocked at his refusal or angry over the rejection.

She stepped close to him and he could smell her perfume and sweat and something close to a shiver worked through his rangy frame. She placed her hands on his chest and let them drift towards the center then back again. Coming up on her toes, she leaned towards his lips.

He pushed her back, and the shocked look on her face became a fierce scowl.

'What the hell's the matter with you? I ain't never had a fella push me away.' She stepped towards him again.

He held up a hand. 'Don't, I ain't a particularly virtuous man.'

She stopped short and laughed. Heat flushed into his cheeks.

'Why the hell you laughin'?'

'That's right funny, Ladigan. Ain't never met a virtuous fella before. You must be the only one in the whole of Colorada.' She slapped her thighs.

'Ain't that funny.'

'Is to me. Maybe you just don't like girls. You one of them types?' She put a healthy measure of accusation into the remark, one that might have come from bruised pride or just plain meanness. He reckoned it was likely a measure of both.

His temper rose. 'Now wait just a damn–'

His words snapped short as blinding pain exploded in the back of his head. He heard

Prilla let out a squawk of fright but his vision went full of stars and the ground rushed towards his face. He barely got his arms out in front of himself to break the fall before hard earth mashed his features into a pulp.

Senses whirling, he rolled over, clutching at the back of his head. Wetness there, but not a lot, more just singing agony.

Something had hit him, hit him hard. He tried to gain his feet. The world cascaded around him, streaks of campfire light and blackness, moonshine and smeared stars. He fell back to the ground, legs refusing to work right.

Hands gripped his gunbelt and yanked it from his waist. Sharp pain from his right side snapped his senses clear. The pain had come from a boot toe and as his gaze rose he saw two men standing over him, their faces grinning masks of intent. The same two men in the crowd in town, men likely working for Timm.

He'd made a serious miscalculation, thinking Timm would not bother with them tonight, but he just didn't figure the son of a gold tycoon would be much more than a pampered rich boy. That was mistake number two tonight.

'Well, well, Ladigan, ain't so tough without

your piece now, are you?' one of the men said. The fella was average-sized, but had chipped teeth, a cauliflower ear and the brow of a fighter. Ladigan focused on the man after throwing a glance about the campsite and seeing no sign of Prilla.

'Don't worry about your lady friend,' the second man said, tone mocking. He was roughly the same size as the other, with sandy blonde hair, but a face unblemished by past collisions with fists. Both held thick pieces of branch and Ladigan knew what had collided with the back of his head. 'She run off, but we'll catch up to her and send your respects after we're done with you.'

The night was getting all-fired better by the minute. After rescuing a saloon girl and getting himself into deep dung with the town bully, she had run off and left him to answer for her freedom. He reckoned he couldn't blame her; though it irked him. But right now he had bigger worries.

The men grabbed at him, each taking an arm and hauling him to his feet. He could barely stand, pain splintering from his side and the back of his head in concert.

One of the men dropped his branch, then wrapped his arms around Ladigan's chest with a vise-grip that pinned his arms to his sides. The other man, the one who looked like a fighter, buried his branch club in Ladigan's gut.

Ladigan tensed his stomach the moment the thing started in motion but it didn't help a whole hell of a lot. Pain rang through his belly and the man swung again before Ladigan could recover.

With the blow, nausea surged and it was all he could do to keep from hurling beans into his attacker's face.

The man let loose a gleeful laugh and drew back for a swing at Ladigan's face, clearly intending to brain him.

On instinct, Ladigan snapped his head back viciously. The impact brought a considerable explosion of pain from where he'd been previously hit, but also a howl of agony from the man holding him. The fellow's nose flattened, then blew out a spray of crimson.

In nearly the same movement, Ladigan thrust his head down and to the side. The swinging club glanced from his ear and sailed past into the already paining face of his attacker.

The man let go of Ladigan with a second bleat of pain and dropped like a sack of potatoes, writhing on the ground.

'Jesus H., Burgis!' the man howled.

The man called Burgis stared at his fallen comrade with a dumbfounded look, club hanging from his hand.

'Christamighty, Linch, I didn't mean–'

His words turned into a muffled curse as Ladigan's foot swept out, boot toe hooking a burning branch from the camp-fire and sending it through the air in a whirling dervish of sparks and streaking light. It hit Burgis in the chest. The man squealed, dropping his club and slapping at the sparks that threatened to ignite his shirt.

Ladigan sprang forward, hurling himself into the man and knocking him off his feet. He landed atop Burgis and quickly made an effort to pound his brains out with a fist.

Ladigan discovered that his impression the man had been a fighter was indeed the case, because Burgis took three straight blows and suddenly roared like a cornered bear. He retaliated with a clubbing left that banged into Ladigan's right ear. Ladigan lost all sensation of hearing anything but a thundering roar and his balance deserted him.

Burgis shoved him free and scrambled to get to his feet. Ladigan fell to hands and knees, shaking his head, trying to clear the cobwebs.

The man called Linch was crawling on the

ground, moaning like a woman in labor.

Ladigan got his senses back just in time to see the fighter lunge at him. He rolled as Burgis came down on him, barely avoiding the full brunt of the impact. He jammed a fist into the man's throat, raked a boot along the fellow's shin. Burgis uttered harsh gagging sounds and instinctively clawed at his damaged windpipe.

Ladigan followed up with a sharp open-fingered jab to the man's left eye and the man howled, losing all desire to fight. Rolling him off, Ladigan scrambled away, leaving the man curled in the dirt.

'Sonofabitch!' Burgis yelled, hand going to his injured eye. 'The sonofabitch done poked my eye out!'

An exaggeration, though Ladigan doubted the man would have much vision there for a spell, perhaps ever.

Ladigan crawled sideways, pushed himself up against the deadfall. Linch, who had come to his feet, took a step towards him, unsteady, but plainly figuring he was in better shape than Ladigan. He gripped a fist-sized rock in his right hand.

Ladigan's gunbelt lay only a few feet away. As the man came towards him, swinging the rock, Ladigan let himself fall sideways.

The rock missed and Linch's momentum carried him straight over the deadfall. He landed with a heavy thunk and immediately tried to right himself, cursing.

Burgis, reaching his feet, staggered into motion, plodding towards Ladigan, murder on his face.

Ladigan snatched at his gunbelt, jerked it close and yanked his Peacemaker from the holster. He swung it up and Burgis stopped short, apparently the vision in his other eye working just fine. Linch froze, too, gasping for breath and eyeing Ladigan, as if debating his chances of taking the Colt away and turning it against him.

'Ain't been done...' Ladigan said, guessing the man's intent. He feathered the trigger for emphasis. He could aim damn near without looking, and despite a slight unsteadiness of his hand at the moment, the bullet buried itself in the ground a fraction of an inch from Linch's left foot.

The man stood rigid, fear jumping across his features.

Ladigan climbed to his feet, gun steadying.

'Get the hell out of here. And tell Jack Timm he ever tries a stunt like this again and I'll send you back to him in the back of a buckboard with holes 'tween your eyes.'

Both men glared, but began backing away. Loyalty didn't mean getting shot full of lead.

They vanished into the woodland and he heard the sounds of them scurrying through the brush like spooked rabbits.

Pain radiated from every corner of Ladigan's body. He snatched up his gunbelt, more than a little annoyed with himself for letting two men sneak up on him. Mistake number three tonight. How many more before he wound up with buzzards picking at his eyeballs?

He strapped on the belt, tied the holster to his thigh with the leather thong, then reached for the bandanna usually at his neck, realizing after a moment he'd given it to Prilla, who'd left it at the sawbones's office. Going to his saddle-bags, he pulled out an old cloth that surrounded a tintype. He glanced briefly at the picture, a likeness of himself and his brother, taken at Tom's twenty-fourth birthday. That flop-eating grin on Tom's face. That was the way Ladigan recollected his younger sibling, that and his brother's strength of character. Tom got the brains and the morals, least in Ladigan's estimation. He'd always admired him for that, admired him for a lot of things. Funny, how brothers could be completely different. Tom had a head on his

48

shoulders, though he often left his good sense in his saddle-bags when he got excited over something. Ladigan had never let anything get in the way of his own good sense on a case – least until tonight.

He shoved the tintype back into the bag and went to the stream, kneeling beside it. Soaking the cloth, he dabbed at the blood on the back of his head.

'Give it to me...' a soft voice came from behind him and he turned to see Prilla standing there, her hand out.

'Why'd you come back?' His head whirled a bit, vision jumping, but she was a sight for sore eyes.

'Nowhere else to go.'

He grunted a reply but handed her the cloth and she leaned down, gently swabbing the back of his head and cleaning away the blood.

'Ain't much of a cut,' she said. 'Head wounds always bleed like hell, though.'

'I reckon.' He paused, irritation coming back. 'That how you show your appreciation, by runnin' off the minute trouble comes?'

'I couldn't have helped none anyway.' A note of hurt hung in her tone and he almost laughed. Who would have thought a whore could get her feelings hurt?

49

'Reckon you couldn't have.'

She finished with the cloth, then knelt beside him and rinsed it in the stream. He stood, the scent of her perfume and womanly musk making some of the pain in his head wane and other things creep into his mind, things he had no call entertaining.

Going to the fire, he lowered himself next to the flames and breathed in the sweet fragrance of burning wood. He lay back, gingerly settling his head against his saddle.

Prilla wrung the water from the cloth and found a branch one of the attackers had used for a club. She jammed the sharp end into the ground near the fire and hung the cloth over it to dry. She went to the deadfall and gathered the blanket around herself, then sat, warming her hands.

'You're free to go about your business.' Ladigan half-hoped she would just walk off, half-prayed she wouldn't. He'd been alone on the trail from Texas for too long and having company, even a fallen woman's, was better than another night trapped in thoughts.

'Like I told you, got nowhere to go.'

'Suit yourself. I'll fetch a hotel tomorrow. You're welcome to come with me or stay here, whatever's your mind.'

'You won't get a room.' She said it with

such conviction he wondered if she weren't right. He hadn't expect Timm to send those men after them tonight and going into the lion's den might mean inviting more trouble.

'I'll get a room,' he assured her, more from a desire to be contrary than actual confidence.

'Pfft.' She made the sound come out as if it said he was a damned fool for even thinking it. 'You reckon Timm won't send those men back tonight?'

'Ain't likely. They'll be in no mood to get their balls handed to 'em a second time so soon.'

She peered at him and he fought the urge to shiver. In the glow of the firelight she looked prettier than he had thought on first sight. Or maybe he was just getting randier.

'You fought them good, Ladigan. Never seen a man try so hard before, least not round these parts.'

So she had stayed close enough to watch the fight and see who came out on top.

'You ain't seen good...' He looked up at the stars, then closed his eyes. Before long, sleep sent the pain away.

In the dark of the alley beside the sawbones' office, Burgis and Linch staggered to a halt.

51

Burgis still held a hand over his bloody eye while Linch probed tentatively at his bashed nose. An egg glowed livid on his forehead where Burgis's club had struck.

Jack Timm stepped from the shadows, taking a long drag on a cheroot. A bandage enwrapped his hand.

'Where's the girl?' Ice glazed Jack Timm's voice. Burgis and Linch exchanged worried glances. 'You were s'posed to bring her back.'

Burgis shifted feet and hung his head a minute. Linch looked away, guilt on his face.

'I asked you gents a question.' Jack Timm tossed down his cheroot and ground it out under a boot-toe. 'Reckon it wouldn't be wise to make me ask it again.'

Burgis' hand lowered from his bloody eye.

'She runned off when we attacked Ladigan.' His voice quavered and he flinched, as if expecting a blow.

Jack Timm's expression didn't change.

'Why didn't you round her up? She's a whore, she couldn't have got far.'

Burgis glanced at Linch, then back to Timm.

'We runned into a little trouble.'

Timm gave a slow nod.

'I can see that. Ladigan?'

Linch's head bobbed.

'We snuck up on him, but he…'

'But he what?' Fury churned in Jack Timm's belly at his men's incompetence. They had been given a job to do and had failed miserably.

'He was tougher than we thought. He got to his gun and threatened to kill us.'

Timm's eyes glittered with violent light.

'Don't expect to be paid this week, maybe next, 'less you got a notion to debate it with me?'

The relieved looks on their bloodied faces said they were thankful to get away with no worse punishment and weren't about to argue the point.

'We need to see the doc, Jack.' Burgis's hand went back to his eye, as if he were afraid the orb would drop out. Jack Timm wondered what Ladigan had done to him. Both looked as though they'd tangled with a wildcat.

'Doc had to go out of town suddenlike. Ain't likely he'll be back. Have Cherish fix you up. Tell her I told you to see her but don't let the old man or that worthless butler get wind of it, 'less you want more than an eye missing…'

Burgis and Linch nodded in unison, then shuffled from the alley. Jack Timm watched them go, wondering just what kind of a man this Ladigan was that he could somehow get the upper hand on two men who could have fought any other man in the town and come out on top. Burgis and Linch were tough *hombres* usually. A curiosity, this man, and Jack needed to dig deeper into his past. He had expected John Ladigan to be more like the brother, but they were very different. The brother wasn't a fighter, but Ladigan ... Ladigan might be more a problem than Jack figured.

His curiosity faded, replaced by fury again. John Ladigan would not run from Timmervale. No, he would be back, and likely soon. When he came, he would find no welcome. Jack would make certain the fella would learn a Timm wasn't to be trifled with. Violence wasn't the answer, at least not immediately. Men like Ladigan had to be broken like a renegade horse, its will crushed until it submitted to the control of its master.

How much did Ladigan know? Jack doubted the man had all the answers or any, else he would have come into Timmervale hell-bent with a county marshal. Ladigan was still in the dark mostly and that pleased Jack, pleased him immensely. It made his cat to Ladigan's mouse so much more delightful.

He strolled from the alley, lighting another cheroot as he headed for the saloon. His session with Prilla had been interrupted but he wouldn't go the night without a woman, one who didn't know the meaning of the word no. He hoped he could still hit hard enough with the bandage on his hand...

CHAPTER THREE

John Ladigan saddled his bay and rode towards Timmervale. After downing another can of cold beans for breakfast, he'd splashed stream water into his face to startle the sleep out of his eyes. Casting a sideways glance at the sleeping form of the bar dove curled up next to the smoldering fire, he'd wondered if she'd be there when he got back, but gave it little thought. Like she told him, she had nowhere to go. He was likely stuck with her a spell. The thought didn't irk him as much as it should have. Maybe he'd spent too many years alone, or maybe what burned as a dim suspicion in his gut was changing the way he felt about not needing anyone in his life.

John Ladigan was a man with few friends

and too many worthless acquaintances. Least that's what any member of the Cattlemen's Association would have claimed had anyone cared to ask. Damn few did. Most found the less they knew of John Ladigan's private details the better for their personal health. Because if they knew a lick about his comings and goings he was likely on their trail for rustling, robbery or murder.

Deadliest manhunter in Texas, was the reputation some damn dime novel scribe with an overactive imagination accredited to him. Some he disarmed, some buried. Although he had killed his share of men, he couldn't say it made him proud. He couldn't say he lost sleep over it either. A job, was all it was.

Least until he set out from Texas for Timmervale.

Questions in his mind, questions that possibly started even before he received the second telegram, the one giving him reason to come to Colorado. Questions, wonders, ponderings. Was manhunting all there was? Did he still have what it took? Did killing ghosts over and over quell any of the burning grief seared into his soul?

The more he brought it to mind, the more he reckoned he simply found the nights on the trail under the stars, alone with his thoughts, was what pleased him. Not the chase, nor the thrill of bringing them to justice. Truth be told, that never did excite him; he did it because something inside made him do it, something born on a fateful day long ago.

Well, perhaps not the alone part. Alone wasn't something he'd given any thought before ... before that second telegram filled him with a denied dread that he suddenly might be irrevocably alone. Forever.

Tom had always been there, far back as he could remember. Younger, but more level-headed, a shepherd of sorts to an elder brother who grew up with a simmering bitterness in his heart and thinly veiled hatred for a God who had seen fit to smite a ten-year-old boy's folks and leave him crying in the dust. His pa hadn't been there to guide him, teach him ranch duties and set him on the path his father and his father's father before him had taken. Not there to rein in a seething temper and untamed sense of righteousness. It had taken Tom to do that, a task that never should have fallen upon an eight-year-old.

But fate was a bastard. The Ladigans had carved a fine reputation as cattlemen in Texas, but that all perished on a blistering

sunny day when bandits rode in and murdered his ma and pa while he and Tom sat in
a one-room schoolhouse getting book-
learned. With two gunshots the Ladigan
legacy ended. Bang, bang, blood soaking
dust. He hadn't been there but could still
hear the gunshots in his mind. And screams.

He hadn't been there. Tom assured him it
wouldn't have mattered, because had they
been home that morning four bodies would
have ridden out in the back of a wagon
instead of two. It was no comfort, but he
knew Tom was right. It hadn't stopped the
fever of revenge for hardcases and their kind
from festering inside, a fever that fashioned
him into the man whom that pulp writer
called an 'avenger', a fella who delivered 'the
hot lead of justice'. Flowery language, that,
but he supposed it fit as well as any.

Tom was different. Tom never carried the
hate inside. He had taken to religion at the
orphanage, something Ladigan never cottoned to. God was one thing, religion was another, and neither seemed good for anything
but mocking the existence of those left
behind.

'God isn't responsible, John,' his brother
kept saying. 'Those men are.' The hell *He*
ain't, Ladigan had thought, but Tom was

right, at least in part.

Those men *were* responsible. Those men and their kind. Those men had to pay, but those men were never found. That fact galled him until it robbed him of sleep too many nights to count, robbed him of rational thought. Those men got away, but since he learned to shoot and track many others had not.

He admired his brother, more than any man in the West, and while he was tempered he wasn't a copy of Tom. He'd developed an almost radical desire to help others who couldn't help themselves, bring to justice those who preyed on others. He figured that afforded him some measure of redemption for failing his kin.

Tom said he was proud of his elder brother, and the feeling was mutual. Tom was aiming to become one of the best newspaper reporters in the country, and if the telegram in Ladigan's saddle-bags was any indication that day wasn't far off.

Something big, the telegram said. What it was, Ladigan had no idea, but it involved Timmervale and its first family somehow.

That was why stumbling on to Jack Timm cutting that whore had given him such a surprise. What had started out as disgust for just another bully preying on the weak had exploded into something that put him in direct conflict with the reason he'd come here.

He shifted in the saddle, feeling the gentle swaying of the big bay beneath him. A brassy sun chased away the chill of the night and glinted from the Winchester snug in its saddleboot. Spruce, fir and lodgepole pine flanked either side of the trail and the air carried a damp sweetness, fragrant as perfume.

The trail widened, opening into town. Timmervale was a sprawling array of shops and buildings, most lining the wide main street. Deep ruts grooved the throughway, and the musky scent of manure and soil hung in the air. A mercantile, dressmaker, gunshop, as well as myriad businesses lined the left side, while a saloon, marshal's office, cabinet maker and lawyer's office stood to the left. The window of a building across from the marshal's carried gilded lettering that said: Timmervale *Gazette*. A few early risers tramped along the boardwalks, some casting him looks then quickly averting their gazes. He recognized a handful from last night.

Timmervale. A town built by the Timms, owned and ruled by the Timms. Damn few hadn't heard of Solomon Timm's luck striking gold and silver. The man owned the largest mines in the Territory, and rumor went he hadn't come across all of them by pure good fortune. Whispers of swindled prospectors and screams of claim jumps dogged Solomon Timm like stink on a skunk. Nothing proven, likely because Solomon Timm always bought the highest-priced lawyers to see to it dung never stuck to his fine leather boots.

Solomon Timm, from what Ladigan knew, was a ruthless businessman with many men in his gilded pockets. That made him like a hundred others who came to power out West but did it make him anything worse? Did he even figure in whatever Tom had discovered?

Ladigan uttered a curse under his breath, wishing his brother had seen fit to provide him with more information, at least provided him with more of a starting point, but Tom couldn't risk passing too much by telegram, not from this town.

What about Jack Timm? Could he be at the focus of Tom's message? Or was he simply another spoiled rich boy with a hankering to cover the fact his pistol wasn't big enough? Did his violent temper go beyond abusing whores and sending men to beat the hell out of the stranger who'd stuck his nose in Timm business?

Ladigan reckoned it wouldn't be long before he found out.

Where are you, Tom?

The question rose in his mind and burning dread took hold of his belly again. He got little chance to think on it. A sound caught his attention and his gaze traveled to the saloon, half a block down.

Two men struggled with a body wrapped in a sheet, endeavoring to haul it down the outside stairway. The man on the bottom dropped his burden, which hit with a heavy thud, likely the body's head. A sick feeling welled in the pit of Ladigan's stomach. The men were being none too respectful, so he reckoned the body must belong to one of the saloon girls.

The man lifted the end of the wrapped body and they started down again. After hurling the corpse into the back of a wagon, one jumped in beside it while the other climbed into the driver's seat and took the reins. The buckboard clattered off.

Ladigan watched it ride for the end of town, until he heard a door shut behind him. He shifted in his saddle to see Marshal Pierson stepping out in the morning sunlight, yawning.

The marshal cast Ladigan a look that said

he was none too happy to see him riding back into town. The look came with a question: What the hell kinda balls you got coming into Timm Territory?

'Why you back here?' Pierson's tone came with a challenge, but an impotent one. A dimestore lawman who enforced his business only when a Timm told him to, Ladigan figured. Pierson stepped off the boardwalk and sauntered up to Ladigan's bay.

'Got business in this town, Marshal. Rather that wasn't a problem.' He figured he'd lay his cards down, see if the marshal had a better hand.

'Take some advice – Ladigan, did you say your name was?'

Ladigan gave a short nod, keeping his gaze locked with Pierson's.

'You best take your business elsewhere and let the fine folks of Timmervale be getting about theirs.'

No threat in the man's tone, maybe even a note of concern.

'Just what is that business, Marshal? Cutting ears off innocent women or disrespecting the dead?'

The marshal raised a puzzled eyebrow, then his gaze went to the saloon, light dawning in his eyes.

'Just a whore who got cut up. How much respect you think she needs?'

Ladigan shrugged.

'Same as anyone else, I'd expect. Where they taking her?'

'Somewhere outside of town. They'll dump her for the buzzards, I imagine.'

Ladigan wasn't sure whether the marshal was serious but if he were joking it was in damn poor taste.

'What happened to her?'

'Like I said, got cut up.'

'What the hell does that mean, Marshal?' The man's attitude was quickly wearing Ladigan's nerves thin.

'What the hell do you mean what the hell does it mean?' The marshal damn near tripped over the words and Ladigan decided the lawdog wasn't being deliberately deceptive; he was just plain stupid.

'She get in a fight with another gal or did Mr Timm decide to cut more than an ear off this time?'

That question sobered the marshal and a dark look crossed his eyes.

'Look, Ladigan, I got nothing against you, but I'm here to tell ya, don't be saying things like that about the Timms if you plan on ridin' out of here in one piece.'

'You sayin' what happened to that girl might happen to me?' His eyes narrowed and the marshal licked his lips and shuffled feet. The man might be under Timm's thumb but he wasn't a brave sort.

'I ain't sayin' nothin' of the sort.' He was, his voice made it plain, but he wasn't about to state it outright.

'Some girls end up that way, Ladigan. Whorin's a rough business and most of them girls wind up dead sooner or later, maybe even by their own hand. I figure this one just couldn't take it no more and slit her throat.'

'You see the body?'

'Didn't have to.'

Ladigan suddenly recollected Prilla mentioning something about girls winding up dead.

'How many?'

'How many what?'

'How many girls gone and slit their own throat lately?'

The marshal shifted feet.

'First one, I reckon.' He was lying again; the tremor in his voice gave him away.

'Not what I heard.'

'You heard wrong.'

Ladigan let a small smile filter onto his lips. He let the subject drop. He hadn't come here looking for whore-killers, though he had half a mind to look into it just to annoy the marshal.

He reached into his pants pocket and pulled out a folded piece of paper. Flicking it open, he held it in front of the marshal's face, who stared at the likeness drawn onto the yellowed sheet.

'You seen this man recently?'

'No.' He answered too fast, Ladigan thought. He answered too fast because he had seen him, if not recently then at some point in the past.

'But you've seen him in town before, Marshal, haven't you.' Ladigan's expression said he would brook no lying.

The marshal shifted feet again and took a deep breath.

'I s'pose he's been in town before. Looks like lots of fellas who come through here.'

'Jack Timm show him the same hospitality he showed me?'

'The Timms treat this town right well, Mr Ladigan. Best keep that in mind.'

'You didn't answer my question.'

The marshal blew out a long sigh.

'Just what is it you came here for, Mr Ladigan? Just who are you and why is it you want to go sticking your hand in a woodpile filled with snakes?'

Ladigan reckoned that was the most honest thing the marshal had come out with since they started talking.

'I came here for business, Marshal, just like I told you. And I ain't afraid of snakes.'

'You best be, Ladigan. You can't never tell which one's poison.'

Ladigan let out a small laugh and shifted in the saddle.

'You recommend the hotel?'

The question plainly annoyed the marshal and Ladigan got a measure of satisfaction out of it.

'Unlikely anyone will welcome you in this town, Mr Ladigan. I recommend a hotel in Wellerville, next town over. They're right friendly folk there.'

'Don't have business in Wellerville, Marshal. Got it here.'

Exasperation crawled over the marshal's gaunt face.

'Mr Ladigan...' He drew out the name. 'What will it take to convince you different?'

'Finding the man in this picture.' He folded the paper and stuck it back into his pocket. He tightened his grip on the reins. 'You'll excuse me, I got that business to attend to.' He reined around and steered the horse towards the saloon, leaving the marshal staring after him.

He sat the bay in front of the saloon, dismounted and tethered the animal to the hitch rail. The place served breakfast, the sign boasted, so he reckoned that would be the place to start. Barkeeps were known gossips.

Pushing through the batwings, the scent of fried eggs and stale whiskey assailing his senses, he noted a few early morning patrons downing their food, faces glazed with indifference. No one gave him more than a glance.

A few bargirls doubled as waitresses, dressed a bit more conservatively for the breakfast hours.

Sunlight slanted through the grime-coated windows, making the room gloomy, and dust danced within the amber shafts. He made his way to the bar and set his Stetson on the counter top. The barkeep carried the same none-too-pleased expression as the marshal.

'We stopped serving breakfast.' The 'keep grabbed a glass and began wiping it out with a cloth.

'Ain't that a coincidence. Give me a whiskey, then.'

'It's six in the a.m.' The man's brow furrowed.

'Never to early to get a start on the evenin'.' No humor came with Ladigan's words.

'We ran out of whiskey.' The 'keep moved off and stuck the glass beneath the counter.

Ladigan hadn't wanted the drink anyway but it told him someone had likely ordered the man not to serve any strangers; he bet that man's name was Timm.

Ladigan slid from the stool, plucking the Stetson from the counter and shoving it on his head. He fished out the folded paper and walked to the end of the bar. Cornering the barkeep, he laid the paper on the chipped countertop.

'You seen this fella?'

The burly man glanced at the drawing.

'No, reckon I haven't. That all you wanted to know?' An edge of irritation honed the man's tone. Ladigan judged him to be of sturdier stock than the marshal, but just as unlikely to co-operate. This man was no coward, but he knew who ran this, town. He wouldn't betray Jack Timm, even if Ladigan shoved a gun barrel against his forehead.

Ladigan folded the paper and pushed it back into his pocket. He held the man's gaze a moment.

'You got a murdered girl taken out the back a few minutes ago.'

An expression of unease crept over the 'keep's round features.

'Who said she was murdered? Damn whore got sick of livin' and cashed in her chips, that's all.'

Ladigan had said it just to see what effect it would have on the man and he reckoned he'd hit the jackpot. The dove'd been murdered. It was no suicide. He wondered if the killing had any connection with Tom's big story.

'Just how many girls cashed their chips lately?' He studied the man's face, waiting for any sign of a lie.

'Happens from time to time. Who keeps count? They're just whores.'

Ladigan stifled a measure of irritation.

'Seems a common belief in this town.' He would get nothing from this man, at least not at this point. 'Obliged for your help.' He didn't mean it and the 'keep knew it, but said nothing.

He moved away from the bar, conscious of the man's gaze following him. He singled out one of the women serving a table and approached her, pulling out a roll of greenbacks.

'I'll pay for you and a bottle, one hour. How much?' The bartender wouldn't break easy, but a dove might. They were notorious talkers once liquored.

'So early in the morning, gent?' The girl, a hard-looking woman barely north of her teens with too much coral on her cheeks and smudged kohl around her eyes gave him a coy smile. Her hand went to her neck in a playful gesture.

'Never too early, I figure. Let's you and me go upstairs.' He pocketed the money.

She smiled but the expression suddenly dropped from her face. She shook her blonde head.

'Sorry, mister, I got other customers.' She backed off and hurried to another table, glancing up with a nervous look, first at him, then towards the bar.

When Ladigan turned, the bartender gave him a smug expression that carried a clear warning: don't try to get information out of any girl here again.

Ladigan tipped his finger to his hat and headed for the batwings, irritated at his lack of success. He'd seen towns sewn up tight before, but this one was a regular virgin's corset.

Stepping out onto the boardwalk, he glanced down the street, eyeing the hotel, now debating the likelihood of getting a room in light of the cool reception he

71

received. What if Prilla was right? Even if he'd got a room would it place them in more danger? Out in the open the camp would be easy enough to ambush, so did it matter?

Deciding it didn't, he made his way to the hostelry, boots thudding in hollow rhythm along the boardwalk. The door shrieked as he opened it, hinges badly in need of lubricating. The place wasn't posh but appeared better kept than some he'd been in. Comfortable enough, with a small sitting-room to one side and a long stairway leading upstairs flanking the west wall. He approached the counter where a frail man in a green visor had his head buried in the registry.

'I need a room.' Ladigan pulled out his roll.

'Week in advance and sign the registry, Mr...?' The clerk looked up and began to turn the book.

'Ladigan.'

The clerk stopped the book short, a startled look jumping on to his features.

'What'd you say your name was?'

'John Ladigan.'

The man licked his lips and his eyelids fluttered. He was a butterfly of a man, Ladigan decided, one about to fly away.

'Sorry, we're full up.' He stuttered, voice quivering.

'Weren't full up just a second ago.' Ladigan's eyebrow cocked.

'My mistake, sorry, Mr Ladigan. I made a mistake, yes sir. We – we're full, I just forgot with the rush and all.'

Ladigan glanced about the lobby, seeing no one.

'Quite a crowd.'

'We're full up, sir. Please, please go elsewhere. I'm sorry, truly.'

Ladigan saw no point in hassling the clerk further. He shoved the roll of greenbacks into his pocket and let out an exasperated sigh. The pattern was clear: Jack Timm had spent time instructing the businesses of this town to refuse any patronage from a man named John Ladigan. He rightly couldn't blame them. They were plumb scared of, or plumb dependent on the Timms.

Ladigan eyed the man, then pulled the drawing from his pocket, flipping it open.

'Seen this man?'

'N-no, I swear I haven't. Handsome fella, though.'

Ladigan decided the clerk was too frightened to lie about it.

'Yeah, that he is.' He folded the sheet and tucked it back in his pocket.

'Looks a lot like you,' the clerk added.

Ladigan nodded. 'Reckon he does.' He turned and headed for the door, frustration tying a knot in his gut. He'd spent all of half an hour in town only to discover one murdered bargirl, no leads and a community living in fear and domination.

Stepping out into the glaring sunlight, he stopped, a surge of adrenaline igniting his defenses as a voice broke his reverie.

'Morning, Mr Ladigan. Fine morning, wouldn't you say? Finding the hospitality in this town not quite what it should be?'

Ladigan's gaze locked on Jack Timm, who stood leaning against a post holding up a wooden awning. A cheroot dangled from his thin lips. He took a deep drag and let the smoke run from the right corner of his mouth. Attired in fancy trousers and a brocade vest with a gold watch chain looping from a pocket, his gray eyes narrowed into a squint against the sun and held steady on Ladigan.

'Like to say I'm surprised to see you, Timm...' Ladigan's voice remained steady, concealing any measure of apprehension he might have felt. Truth to tell, seeing the man standing there so calmly took him aback slightly. He hadn't expected to run into Timm for a spell after last night. In the back of his mind he figured the boy would hang back, stay out of range, and have others do his dirty work. Another mistake.

The surprise didn't last long. The confidence and steel nerves forged by years of manhunting quickly took control. Ladigan stepped towards the man, alert but relaxed, ready for any sudden moves Timm might make for the gun at his waist. He tried to size him up further but got conflicting notions. Was Timm a coward who beat whores? Or was he a mad dog ready to spring at the slightest provocation?

'You plan on startin' something in full view of witnesses, Mr Timm?' Ladigan's voice held a challenge and he half-hoped the man would go for his gun.

Timm let out a chopped laugh, gazed out at the street and took another drag on his cheroot.

'What would I start, Mr Ladigan? I reckon a manhunter like yourself would be more than ready for any move I might make. Or would hired killer be more accurate?'

'You know who I am?' The fact didn't surprise him.

'I do now. Didn't take much effort to learn the facts about John Ladigan, most famous bounty man out of Texas.'

'Then you know why I'm here...'

'Do I?' Timm raised an eyebrow and looked directly at him. ''Fraid not, Mr Ladigan, unless it's to save the poor downtrodden bargirls of Timmervale. How is Prilla, by the way? Treatin' her well?'

Ladigan suppressed the urge to knock him off the boardwalk. Barely.

'Didn't try to cut off one of her ears, at any rate.'

A flash of annoyance in Timm's gray eyes.

'Very good, Mr Ladigan. Woman like her needs all her parts, don't you agree?' He smiled without humor, tossed the cheroot to the boardwalk and ground it out under a heel.

'Stay away from her, Timm. I won't tell you twice.'

A slight scoffing sound came from his lips.

'A threat, Mr Ladigan? I would have thought you above such things.'

'No threat, just friendly advice. Think it over the next time you decide to send your men after me.'

'Don't know what you're talking about, sir.' He lied without a hitch in his voice, but a surreptitious glance gave him away. At either end of the boardwalk stood Burgis, a patch over his eye, and Linch, the vicious look on their faces scarcely restrained.

'Those are your men, aren't they?' He ducked his chin towards each.

Timm shrugged.

'They work for me, chores and errands mostly. What they do in their off time is none of my concern.'

'I was under the impression no one in this town has off time where a Timm concerned.'

'Really? Well, you're wrong, Mr Ladigan. Why, just last night I gave the doc some long-deserved rest.'

'What the hell's that s'posed to mean?' A plunging feeling hit Ladigan's belly.

'Told him to take a nice long vacation. Reckon he deserves at least that after years of fine service to this community.'

'Where'd he go?' Ladigan's voice remained steady but the urge to grab the man by the vest and jam him against the post grew nearly overpowering. Jack Timm could count himself damned lucky Tom had taught Ladigan to rein his temper.

'Mexico, I imagine. Maybe California. Don't matter. He won't be back.' The last words came out cold and lethal.

'You go back to the saloon last night, Timm?' Ladigan saw a flicker of something on the man's face but Timm expertly recovered himself again. Sober, Timm had control; half-drunk was another story.

'What are you really asking me, Mr Ladigan?' Timm eyed him with a challenge in his eyes.

'Reckon you know damn well. Also reckon you know I won't give up on the reason I came here, so stay the hell out of my way.' It wasn't subtle but Ladigan found himself growing weary of the cat-and-mouse exchange Timm appeared to enjoy.

'No one will cater to you in this town, Mr Ladigan. You realize that, don't you?' Timm studied him and Ladigan's nerves cinched another notch. 'Yes, I can see you do. Why don't you join the doc in Mexico or California? Hear it's not so cold in those places. Oh, and tell dear Prilla I hope she heals up soon, will you?' A note of mockery laced his tone but something else as well, something that told Ladigan Jack Timm really didn't want him to ride out. It said he wanted revenge, and would enjoy toying with his prey until it was time for the slaughter. Jack Timm wasn't intimidated by the reputation of a famous manhunter, an avenger. He was perversely intrigued with the thought of breaking him. He wasn't a coward, or typical bully; he thrived on domination and John

Ladigan represented something no one else in town could provide him with – a challenge.

Ladigan stepped from the boardwalk, brushing against Timm's shoulder, then casting him a final glance. Both Timm's men started forward, but Timm gave a slight shake of his head, stopping them. The game had changed. Timm had won today's round by frustrating Ladigan, blocking him at every turn and they were even now.

Ladigan was damned unhappy with that. He felt as if he were riding off licking his wounds, Jack Timm smugly watching him go. It was a position he was neither used to, nor enjoyed.

CHAPTER FOUR

Sitting in the saddle, guiding the horse towards camp, Ladigan let out a heavy sigh. The more he dwelled on it the more the stalemate with Jack Timm irked him. He wasn't used to games. He was used to tracking his quarry, then either bringing it in for hanging or shooting it dead.

Was Jack Timm really his quarry? At this

point, Ladigan had no way of telling if the younger Timm had committed a crime for which he would have to answer to a manhunter. At present, Jack Timm was simply a burr in his saddle, and an obstacle to the mystery that had summoned John Ladigan to Timmervale. Ladigan couldn't bring him in for beating a whore, not with the marshal in Timm's pocket, and he couldn't hang him for it. He could saddle an assault charge to the two men working for Timm, but doubted any counsel or jury assembled in Timmervale would bring down a conviction, and it would mean a delay in his mission. Jack Timm would likely welcome the event as part of the game, knowing it would be another round that went to him in the final tally.

So he was stuck with his draw, one round Timm, one round to himself, and no clearcut purpose for continuing the fight, unless he could somehow link either Jack or Solomon Timm to the vanishing of the man on the paper in his pocket.

If that link existed, finding it was problematic. Jack Timm was set to counter every query and move Ladigan chose to make. The strategy played hell with Ladigan's admittedly ambiguous plans. If he were going to accomplish anything he would need to question some of the townsfolk, especially the telegraph operator and newspaper man. If they proved as open with information as the marshal and saloon 'keep, he would get nowhere fast.

Another sigh, and tightening nerves. As he approached the campsite, he slowed the big bay. The sun had jumped a handspan above the horizon and the thin air had warmed enough to bring a trickle of sweat, which snaked down the side of his face. Lark buntings chittered in the forest and the balsamic fragrance of the woodland played in his nostrils.

Again his mind wandered, and a question formed: *Was he losing his edge?*

He'd never questioned his career before, never felt so unsettled and so ... so what? Afraid? Was that it? Was that possible for a man like himself, a man with nerves of steel and a heart of stone? Something had changed after receiving that second telegram. Something that rode the dark suspicion bunched up in his belly telling him he was too late and his life would never be the same. Restlessness, moments of confusion, unbidden questions.

What if it comes down to the worst? What if you lose him?

Did that make everything he had done utterly disposable? Maybe it didn't, but another personal loss would take something he had come to depend on more than he'd realized – the approval of a brother who legitimized humanity, who epitomized strength. It would take a substantial piece of who John Ladigan was and crush it. He reckoned he didn't know for certain whether there would be enough left over to go on.

For an instant he lifted his gaze towards the sapphire sky, and almost said a prayer. It hung on his lips, dying there, as his old cynicism and bitterness crawled up from the depths of his being. No God was going to listen to a man who made killing his living.

Shaking from his thoughts, he steered the big bay towards the stand of cottonwood. A scan of the campsite told him Prilla had woken and was nowhere to be seen. Had she run off again? Why did that notion raise a specter of disappointment? He'd be lucky to be rid of her. Wouldn't he?

Dismounting, he tethered the horse to a branch, then tossed his saddle-bags to the ground and rummaged out a stick of jerky. Chewing it while he stared out at the stream, a noise downstream caught his ear. He gazed in that direction, wondering what the devil had made it. It wasn't the sound of anything posing a threat, but it wasn't the sound of anything natural to the woodland either.

He stuffed the remainder of the jerky into his mouth, and moved to the edge of the tiny clearing. Slipping into the woods, he kept his steps light and avoided rustling clumps of brush. The sound came again. This time, closer to it, he figured out what it was. He paused, peering towards the source.

Prilla huddled on the stream bank, heaving into the water. So she hadn't left after all. He couldn't deny feeling a measure of relief. She retched and he backed away, letting her be. He reckoned either her ear was festering and causing a fever and sickness or her nerves had caught up with from the night before.

Returning the campsite, he sat on the deadfall and waited.

Fifteen minutes later, she returned, face washed pale, steps faltering. She eased herself to the ground before the burned-out camp-fire, then pulled the blanket around her, despite the day's warmth. She rubbed at a spot on her low back, wincing.

'Your back paining?' He didn't let any particular sympathy bleed into his voice. Sympathy was something that came hard for him, least since his parents died. Tom always told him it was no good to be cold to others' pain, no matter what life threw at you, and he tried to keep that in mind. But sometimes he just didn't know how to act, especially with women. He wasn't around common folk all that much, much of his association limited to Cattlemen Association members and forced contact with the hard-cases he hauled back for trial. He got damn little practice at social skills and doubted they'd fit right on a man like him, anyway.

'Paining all over.' Her voice came a hint raspy. 'Fell down the saloon stairs. Got more sore spots than a lizard with a sunburn.'

He almost smiled, but maybe she wasn't trying to be funny. He couldn't tell. Her jaw had turned a ripe shade of purple and he could see some clear leakage on her bandage.

'You sick?'

She eyed him and it wasn't a particularly pleasant expression.

'What makes you ask that?'

'Saw you depositing your guts in the stream. Didn't want to interrupt.'

'You're all heart.'

'You're all rump.' Now why the hell did he go and say something idiotic like that? A wave of heat went through his face and he prayed his embarrassment didn't show.

'You got a thing for skinny women?' Annoyance laced her voice and he didn't know what to say, so he peered ahead at the stream and tried to look more dignified than he felt.

'Just thinkin' maybe your ear is getting mortified.' He lifted himself off the deadfall and retrieved the blue-speckled coffee pot. He needed to do something to get out from under her stare. He filled the pot with stream water, then got the fire going again and set some more willow-bark tea to brewing.

Pulling the blanket tighter about her shoulders, she watched him with detached interest.

'Maybe I need to get the doc to give me some more medicine.'

'If you mean laudanum, it won't help festerin' none. 'Sides, that sawbones won't be doin' anything for you or anyone else.'

'Why not?'

'He left town.'

'Why?'

'Vacation, I'm told.'

Curiosity crossed her face. 'Who told you?'

'Jack Timm.'

The curiosity turned to shock. 'You talked to him?'

'Reckon I did.'

'And he just let you walk away?'

'How's he s'posed to stop me?' He asked it earnestly and she looked at him like he was the world's biggest fool.

'He owns the damn town, least his pa does. He can do whatever he wants.'

'Reckon maybe not. Reckon maybe his pa wouldn't like him tryin' to kill a famous manhunter in front of everyone and attracting unwanted attention.'

She studied him, looking somehow fragile suddenly, paler.

'Solomon Timm crushes men. He don't give a rat's backside who you are.'

'He crushes them in business, but I reckon if he's anything like I heard he doesn't want blood on his hands directly and Jack Timm shooting me in the open would do that.'

She cocked an eyebrow. 'You get the better of Jack?'

His face went red; he felt it, so he turned back to the stream but he knew she had seen it.

'You didn't get whatever you went to Timmervale for, did you? Town didn't welcome you with fresh hot biscuits and warm walnut pie. Told you so, Ladigan. Timmervale's the devil's own town.'

He let out a long sigh and turned to her.

'Went for a hotel room. Manager wouldn't sell. Fact, you're right, folks I talked to weren't what could be considered forth-coming.'

'They're afraid. Everyone who depends on Timm money is afraid. The old man don't come to town. He lets Jack have his way there. He likes folks beholdin' to him. He likes them afraid of him.'

'You afraid of him?'

Anger fleshed in her blue eyes.

'Didn't used to be. I was his favorite.'

'Now?'

She shrugged. 'Not afraid, exactly, just know there ain't no use swimmin' upstream. He's ruined me, likely, and that's what I got to live with.'

'Ruined you?'

Her gaze dropped and she stared at the ground.

'Meant my ear. He ruined my ear.'

She was lying but he let it pass. 'You been with Jack Timm a lot before last night, I take it.' A spike of something hot and unidenti-fiable stabbed his belly as he asked it, though he had no idea why. She was a whore, for chrissakes. Natural she'd been with many men.

'A few times. Like I said, I was his

favorite.' No compunction in her voice, no apology, either.

'He beat you before?'

'Some. Nothin' bad as last night, though.'

'If he beat you, why'd you keep botherin' with him?'

'Wasn't a choice. Jack Timm gets what he wants. He chooses a girl and that's that. Most end up with bruises. One got a broken leg, so I reckon I was lucky.'

'How many got dead?'

She looked up at him. 'Five I know of.'

'By his hand?'

She shook her head. 'Reckon not. Jack Timm likes to control his women, but he leaves them to consider their bruises. Those girls that died ... they all killed themselves, I heard.'

'You believe that?'

'No...' Her voice dropped to nearly a whisper. 'But I don't know Jack would do that.'

'You seemed pretty sure of it last night.'

'Last night I was scared. He wouldn't have killed me, likely.'

'He would have cut your ear clean off.'

'Wouldn't have even done that if I had given him what he wanted.' Her voice lowered and she frowned.

'Right generous of him.'

'Don't matter now.'

'Don't it? Another girl died last night. I saw men carrying her down the back stairs. Slit her own throat, I hear tell from the barkeep. Reckon he knew better.'

She went silent for long moments. The sounds of the stream trickling and shushing whispers of the breeze filled that silence like a dark lullaby.

'Can't do nothin' about it,' she said at last, a hitch in her voice.

He folded his arms, brow furrowing.

'Can't or won't? Last night you begged for help and no one listened. That how you want it to be for the next girl who decides to "kill herself"?'

'That's just the way it is in this town, Ladigan. What makes you so high and mighty, anyway?' Anger flashed in her blue eyes but he heard a ghost of guilt in her voice. 'You're some famous manhunter, you said. That means you kill folks. That don't make you better than no one in that town.'

The accusation pricked him but he didn't let it show. He wondered why he should even give a damn what she thought.

'The men who died deserved it because they killed others. But I don't kill 'em all. Some I just bring in.'

Her gaze locked with his.

'They die then anyway, don't they? Same thing.'

'They do if they're guilty of a crime.'

'So you're a killer either way. You ain't no better than no one in Timmervale.' Her words held little conviction, but got under his skin all the same.

'The hell!' Every muscle tightened and his throat clutched. His heart jumped into a faster beat. 'I saved your rump last night and you defend those folk and Jack Timm?'

'I ain't defendin' them exactly. I–'

'Then what the devil would you call it? They wouldn't have lifted a finger to stop Timm from doing his worst to you and they haven't lifted a finger to stop those other girls from gettin' killed. Way I see it, there's a damn fine line between being afraid and being an accomplice to things a moral man would find despicable. You best decide which side you want to come down on.'

She twisted her lips into a curse and nearly let it fly, but at the last moment simply let out an angry blast of air.

'What the hell you want here in Timmervale anyway, Ladigan? Why you playin' hero and preacher where you ain't wanted?'

His gaze locked on her and he wanted to

tell her she was plain wrong. He was no hero, he was just a man who saw some distinction between right and wrong, a man who carried a burning need to make things better for a few. He wanted to tell her what had made him the way he was, how death and a brother he admired had shaped him into the thing of retribution he'd become. But he didn't. He couldn't. After all these years it was still too white-hot in his soul to share with someone who didn't matter. She was a whore, nothing more, nothing permanent. She had no right to know the measure of a man such as he, and no right to question it.

So why did her words eat at him so?

He dipped into his pocket and pulled out the folded paper, then snapped it open. Holding it before her face, he waited until she took a good long look.

'You seen this fella around town over the past month?'

Eyes narrowing, she studied the paper harder, then shook her head. 'Not to my recollection. Looks a bit like you.'

'He's my brother. I came here to find him.' He folded the paper and stuffed it back into his pocket.

'How you know he came to Timmervale?'

'Got a telegram from him. He wanted to

be the West's most famous reporter, was working on a case, one that involved the Timms somehow, though I don't know in what capacity. Was big, was all he said.'

'So why wasn't he waitin' on you?'

'That's what I'm here to find out. Got a second telegram from someone that led me to believe something might have happened to him.'

Her face softened a measure.

'I ruined it, didn't I?'

'What are you talkin' about?' His tone still held an edge.

'You wanted to come in quiet and find your brother, but I ruined it. You got in trouble savin' me. You should have just ridden on by, Ladigan. That's what I would have done. You're a fool.'

'So you keep tellin' me.' He didn't think he'd ever met anyone as ungrateful as this woman. He reckoned a simple thank you wasn't in her vocabulary. Looking for anything more than an argument from her was likely a waste of time, so he decided to change the subject. 'Come sundown, we best get you to the doc's and some medicine. No point stayin' here in the open.'

Her eyes narrowed. 'Thought you said he left?'

'Did, but his office is still there. Out here we're open targets. I plan to stay at the saw-bones' place where I got four walls around me.'

She laughed, mocking him, and he bristled with irritation. 'When'd you hit on that stroke of genius?'

Just now, he almost said, but refrained. Jack Timm might have won today's round but Ladigan was determined to win the next. That meant taking the fight right into the man's backyard.

'We'll ride out at dusk. I got no doubts we'll get seen at some point, but darkness'll lessen the chances of immediate attention.'

She shook her head. 'You're a damn fool.'

'Stop sayin' that.'

'He might be dead, Ladigan...' Her voice softened, and for a moment he suspected she might have some small shred of decency buried in her lack of tact.

But the words stung and he didn't answer. The dark suspicion in his belly grew stronger and left him brooding for the next few hours.

When dusk came he saddled the horse and stamped out the small fire he'd kept going. Prilla seemed constantly given to chills, no matter the sun had beaten down through the thin air until heat waves shimmered from the ground. She made a number of trips downstream in the morning then slept most of the day.

Before mounting, he double checked his Peacemaker out of habit, sliding it in and out of the holster to make sure it wouldn't snag. Hoisting her up behind him, he heard her groan, though he tried to be as gentle as possible. Her arms went around his waist and he found himself pleased with the feeling, though he reckoned he'd not met a more ornery gal, whore or no.

He set a slow but steady pace, trying to jounce her as little as possible, though after she awoke she seemed stronger, looked less pale. She'd certainly put away enough of his jerky and beans, though whether she'd hold on to them long was a matter of speculation.

Reaching Timmervale, he kept alert for potential trouble, but the streets were quiet. Darkness covered the town, the premature darkness brought by low-hanging clouds hugging the distant Rockies. Shadows shifted in menacing shapes and low-turned outside hanging lanterns did little to dispel the gloom with their anemic light.

The saloon appeared in full swing, light blazing from within, the sounds of a tinkler piano and raucous laughter ringing out. He reckoned there was plenty of reason for the folks of Timmervale to drown their sorrow – and their guilt.

He saw no sign of Jack Timm.

Reaching the doctor's office, he slipped from the saddle and reached up, placing his hands on her hips and lifting her down. He guided his horse around to the alley, then to the back of the livery stable.

'What the hell are you doing?' she asked in a hissing voice.

'Making arrangements for my horse. Don't expect me to leave him in the street all night, do you?'

'Jack will find out we're here. The livery man will tell him. He won't let you keep your horse there anyway, if Timm has anything to say about it.'

'Ain't plannin' to give him a choice. Us being here won't be a secret for long, anyway. Like you said, town's in Timm's pocket. Somebody will see us and tell him, but it ain't likely Timm will strike right off, anyhow. He wants a game of it.'

'What if you're wrong?'

'You get a bandage on the other ear.'

'Ain't funny. You don't know what a man like that can do.'

'I got a notion.'

'You're a fool, Ladigan.'

'Thought I told you to quit sayin' that.'

'Hard to hear without ears.'

'You still got 'em.'

'Not for long, most like.'

'You're free to ride off.'

'Got nowhere to go and no money.'

He glanced at her, and she looked smaller and more dishevelled than she had before. Splotches of blood dotted her peek-a-boo blouse and her skirt was torn in places.

'Tomorrow I'll have the dressmaker sell me something to make you more presentable. Then you can decide if you want to leave.'

'Thought I told you I had nowhere to go?'

'I could think of a place...'

She glared and he almost laughed.

He led his horse into the livery, the glow of lanterns greeting him along with the musky cologne of hay, manure and old leather. A small man came from a back office immediately and looked them over.

'Prilla...' he said, voice disapproving.

'You were a hell of a lot more enthusiastic last time you saw me, Burt...' Ladigan heard spite in her tone.

The livery attendant colored and shifted his gaze to Ladigan.

'Can't board him here. No room.'

Ladigan glanced at a row of empty stalls, then back to the man.

'I see plenty of space. You'll board him. I'll give you a week in advance.' He fished out the roll of greenbacks.

'Don't want your money, stranger. I know who you are and I know I ain't s'posed to take your business. Cain't make it no more clear than that.'

'Jack Timm told you not to do business with me?'

The man didn't say yes but fidgeted and his gaze darted about.

'Please, just leave me be.'

Ladigan forced a cold smile. 'Can't do that, Burt. See, I need my horse attended to and you're going to do it. You're not going to tell Mr Timm either, because we both know he wouldn't like it.' He counted off a number of bills and tossed them on the floor at the man's feet, then pocketed the rest and laid a hand over the butt of his Peacemaker. He was in no mood for yet another of Jack Timm's prearranged obstacles.

A panicked look jumped into Burt's eyes.

'He'll find out. He'll make things tough on me or make me leave town.'

'Way I see it you're caught 'tween a rock

and a barn wall, friend. You take care of this horse and I'll be back in an hour to fetch him. You don't, there'll be hell to pay. I make myself clear?'

The livery man shuddered, licked his lips, but obviously didn't know who was the bigger threat at the moment, Jack Timm or John Ladigan. He gave a stuttering nod, and Ladigan turned and walked out, Prilla trailing him.

'You sure he won't tell Timm?' she asked, as they rounded the alley and came up to the sawbones' office.

'Would you?' He tried the doorhandle, found it unlocked, and shoved the door open. The office was dark, moonlight bleeding through window blinds. It took him a few minutes to locate a lantern and fire it up. He handed the box of lucifers he found on the table next to the lamp to Prilla and she ignited other lamps in each of the three rooms.

Ladigan searched the rooms, noting suits hanging in a closet, a shaving kit on a bureau and personal belongings such as tintypes still placed about.

'Looks like Doc Porter went on his vacation without his belongings.' He went to a small back room, which held a bed, an oversized stuffed chair, bureau and nightstand, upon which rested a porcelain pitcher and wash-basin.

Prilla lowered herself into a chair in the exam room, while Ladigan went to the cabinet and found some carbolic and a fresh bandage. He gently removed the old dressing and examined her wound. He saw some redness and evidence of clear leakage, but nothing festering. It made him wonder why she had been so sick earlier. He cleaned the wound and redressed it, without giving it any more thought.

'What'd you mean when you told that livery man you'd be back in an hour?' asked Prilla, after he finished.

'Just what I said. I ain't letting Timm win the next round. Decided I'm going to have a parley with his father and see if I can't shake loose a lead to my brother.'

She stared at him dumbfounded, mouth hanging open, but no words coming out. He rather preferred it that way but the silence didn't last for long.

'You're a bigger fool than I thought.' She sputtered the words, eyes wide.

'There's that word again.'

'You got a better one?'

'Didn't come here to sit around bein' a

99

target. If Solomon Timm or his son has something to do with my brother's disappearance I'll get it out of them somehow. Never been one for dancing around things.'

'You'll get yourself killed.'

'Nice of you to worry.'

Did she blush? He wasn't entirely sure but it sure as hell looked to him like she did.

'I ain't worried. Just what do you expect me to do here if you get yourself buried?'

'You're all heart...' He made his tone as mocking as possible.

'You're all fool!' She wrapped her arms about herself and gave him her best look of condemnation, but he saw something deeper behind it. At least he thought he did. It was hard to tell with a woman like that.

'Best get some rest while I'm gone.'

'I'll prepare for your funeral.' She was brewing, that was plain. He reckoned he didn't want to be here when the steam exploded from the spout.

Leaving her staring after him, he returned to the livery and retrieved his horse.

He knew exactly where the Timm spread lay. He had passed it coming in, giving it little more than a glance at the time. He rode the trail running from the opposite end of town towards the valley that housed the mansion.

Mansion might have been an understatement. A hulking Victorian thing, Timm must have had it shipped from the East block by block at a staggering expense. It appeared hideously out of place, stuck in the wilds of Colorado. Its loathsome shape loomed ahead, frosted with moonlight, nestled in a grassy expanse peppered by outbuildings that likely served as workers' quarters.

The mansion itself reared up like a castle, great stones and brick, turrets and ornate balconies, exhibiting a majestic grandeur that starkly contrasted with the workman-like simplicity of Timmervale's structures. A castle fit for a Gild King. Ladigan stifled a short whistle. The dwelling cost $5,000 if it cost a gold eagle.

To his surprise, he rode in unmolested, wondering if rifles were trained on him from the lighted windows of an outbuilding. He kept his hands high on the reins and made no sudden moves, though he spotted no one.

Reaching the mansion, he stepped from the saddle and tethered the horse to a post.

His bootfalls sounded abnormally loud as he climbed the stairs and crossed the sprawling piazza. The front door, fashioned of some dark wood thick enough and large enough to guard a fortress, opened before he reached the gilded doorknocker. A wiry man with pinched features, dressed in a black-and-white uniform and an annoyed expression, waited, head slightly upturned. Ladigan noticed the bulge of a gun beneath the man's suitcoat.

'May I ask your business here, sir?' The servant put a condescending emphasis on the word 'sir'.

'I've come to see Solomon Timm.' Ladigan put a healthy measure of command in his voice. 'Reckon we've got business.'

The man raised an eyebrow. 'You have an appointment, *sir?*'

Damn, there was that belittling emphasis again. It pulled his already short nerves tighter.

'I'm seein' him. Tell him I'm here or get the hell out of my way.'

The servant's hand started towards the gun under his coat and Ladigan readied for the draw, but a voice from the interior stopped the man from committing a fatal mistake.

'Show Mr Ladigan in, Gainly.'

'Yes, sir,' said the servant, without turning his head, the annoying condescension instantly gone when addressing whoever had spoken.

Ladigan stepped inside, doffing his Stetson and wondering if Prilla weren't right in her assessment of his being a fool.

Beyond the corner of the house darkness moved. A figure stepped from the shadows, gaze riveted on the man standing in the doorway, bathed in light from the interior. He watched, face hard and gray eyes glittering, as Ladigan went inside and the butler closed the door.

Ladigan. Here. The manhunter had balls, that much Jack Timm had to cede to him. What the hell was he up to?

Earlier today Jack Timm had wallowed in elation over countering Ladigan, but now the manhunter wasn't playing by the rules. Coming here was unexpected. Indeed, this was the last place Jack had figured on seeing him tonight.

Jack knew a great deal about the man. Finding the facts on Ladigan had not proved difficult. His father kept dossiers on nearly all manhunters, in case their services should ever be needed. As a whole, manhunters were a seemly lot, men who hired their guns and did whatever was necessary for a price without asking troublesome questions. Useful to men like Solomon Timm who dealt in cutthroat business practices. Ladigan was different, and his file had been marked as such, the words 'Unacceptable' scrawled across a record of incidents and completed cases that had led to an inordinately high number of convictions. Ladigan was one of a fistful of manhunters who could lay claim to a set of standards; that made him useless to Solomon Timm. It also made him dangerous to have as an enemy.

Jack didn't care for this a lick. Whatever Ladigan was up to Jack wasn't about to have his game ruined by it.

He pulled a cheroot from a silver case that he fished out of his vest pocket and, puffing it to light, took a deep drag, considering his next move. A thin smile appeared on his lips. It was time for those no-goods of his to redeem themselves and show Ladigan he simply could not break the rules as Jack set them.

He went down the steps, keeping his footsteps light and quiet, then walked to one of the outbuildings. Buttery light bled through dusty windows and fell across the porch. Going to the door, he twisted the handle and stepped inside. Two men sat hunched over a small table, cards jammed into their beefy hands. Burgis and Linch sprang to their feet when they realized who had entered.

'Mr Timm, we wasn't expectin' you tonight.' Burgis tossed his cards to the table, face down.

Jack's gaze swept over the two men.

'Ladigan showed up at the main house. You two got a second chance to do things right.'

Neither man looked particularly pleased with the notion and Jack had half a mind to shoot them both on the spot.

'What's he want here?' Burgis asked.

'Don't know yet, but I don't like it. When he leaves follow him. Cut him off half-way to town and break one of his legs. Make sure you do it slowly.'

Both men looked at each other and swallowed hard, but said nothing.

Jack Timm turned, then paused at the door looking out into the moonlit night, his back to Burgis and Linch.

'Don't fail me this time. I'm not likely to take it well.'

'S-Sure thing, Mr Timm,' said Burgis, stammering. 'We'll fix his wagon this time.'

Jack Timm laughed an unpleasant laugh.

'See that you do.'

He stepped out into the night.

Gainly led Ladigan through a vestibule and

down a wide hall to the drawing-room. The room was elegantly furnished with thick velvet draperies of royal blue and polished mahogany furniture with carved legs and ball-and-claw feet. On one wall hung an elegant Persian tapestry, likely brought back from a trip abroad. French paintings adorned two other walls; a gilt-edged harpsichord stood in a corner. A polished bar held an array of liquor decanters and humidors with fine cigars.

Solomon Timm stood at the bay window, gazing out into the night, a sherry glass in one hand, a cigar in the other. A large man, he carried an air of command even with his back turned. Iron-haired, he was attired in an evening suit with close-fitting sleeves, turned-back cuffs and a single-breasted waistcoat sporting a deep V front. A high-collared boiled shirt and braided trousers completed the ensemble. When he turned it was almost as if he expected a genuflection.

'You should have sent word, Mr Ladigan.' A deep rumbling voice, solid with authority. 'I would have had Gainly prepare something for your arrival. It's not often a famous man such as yourself visits Timmervale.'

Ladigan fingered the brim of his Stetson.

'You know who I am?'

Timm took a drag on his cigar, blew smoke out in rings.

'Of course. It's my business to know people. Your pulp novel was quite popular among the miners who work for me.'

'It's your business to know people's weaknesses, don't you mean?'

A glint of irritation sparked in the elder Timm's gray eyes. Likely damn few folks spoke bluntly to this man. Ladigan had come across too many of his type and wasn't about to be intimidated.

Timm shrugged.

'A wealthy man can't be too informed, Mr Ladigan. Such information comes in handy when dealing with unscrupulous schemers who spend their time plotting takeovers.'

Ladigan let a small grin turn his lips.

'The way you took it from them?'

Solomon Timm laughed, the sound booming and somehow contrived.

'I seize opportunities, Mr Ladigan, nothing more. Men too weak to hold onto their claims have no call staking them in the first place.'

'Some might see it different.'

'Not in this town, sir.' He said it with all the authority of a man who was confident he ruled the world, or at least a sizable parcel of

107

it. 'But you didn't come here to debate my business practices, did you? From what I hear you made quite the scene in town?'

Ladigan moved deeper into the room. The sweet fragrance of Timm's cigar smoke drifted into his nostrils.

'Jack tell you that?'

'He didn't have to. I questioned two workers, one of whom's missing an eye now. Seems you attacked them quite unprovoked.'

'They tell you Jack sent them after me?'

The man raised an eyebrow. 'Why would he do that, Mr Ladigan? Jack has no quarrel with you I am aware of.'

'He might. Maybe you should ask him what he gets out of cutting off whores' ears?'

The elder Timm's face darkened, but he quickly covered his displeasure.

'Jack's got some bad habits, I am aware, but he's not a violent man. Boys will be boys, as they say, and I let him have free rein in Timmervale. I have more important matters to attend to.'

'You might ask some of the women at the saloon what they think about Jack. At least the ones who haven't been found with their throats cut.'

Solomon Timm's face darkened another shade. A slow rage burned in his eyes, but he was a man used to holding his cards close to his vest.

'I don't care for what you're insinuating, Mr Ladigan. You have proof of something, present it. If not, don't waste my time.'

Ladigan shrugged.

'No proof, but you best hope I don't find it. I'd hate to have to send you an invitation to a hanging.'

Solomon Timm let out a long breath and went to the bar. He jammed his cigar out in a gold tray and took a deep swallow of his sherry, then set the glass on the counter.

'Why'd you come here, Ladigan. To accuse my son of misdeeds? To blackmail me, so you wouldn't talk? I would have thought you of higher character than that.'

Ladigan almost laughed. He pulled the paper from his pocket and unfolded it.

'I came looking for this man.'

Solomon Timm glanced at the drawing and shook his head.

'No one I've seen. Anything else?'

The man's tone carried a dismissive note and Ladigan knew his welcome had worn out. He folded the sheet and returned it to his pocket.

'Reckon that's it. Also reckon you should tell Jack he best stay out of my way.'

'You presume a lot, Mr Ladigan. I might warn you to stay out of *my* way. If you know anything about me, you know that's no idle request. That man in your drawing hasn't been around here. I recommend you look for him in some other town.'

A sound came from behind him and Ladigan turned to see a woman standing in the entryway. Adorned in an evening gown of sapphire blue with a *cuirasse* bodice that came to a point in front, she presented a vision of loveliness that nearly took Ladigan's breath away. A low *décolletage* was off the shoulder and ornamented with deep lace and velvet *fichu*; short puffed sleeves were trimmed with velvet ribbon and bows, and a trained and flounced skirt and overskirt were embellished in velvet and lace. A diamond choker glittered against the pale flesh of her neck. Blonde hair piled high framed an elegant face with a slightly turned-up nose, deep-blue eyes. Ladigan noticed she used makeup, but not quite enough to cover the ghost of a bruise along one side of her face.

'My wife, Cherish, Mr Ladigan.' Solomon Timm moved towards the woman, who gave Ladigan a slight curtsy. 'We have a previous engagement, so if you would be so kind...' He gestured towards the door as Gainly seemed to appear out of nowhere.

Ladigan nodded, walking towards the hall, but paused beside Cherish Timm. Her perfume filled his nostrils and close up the bruises looked deeper, though they had likely happened a week or more previously. They reminded him of the one on Prilla's jaw and he took the notion that mistreating women ran in the Timm blood.

She smiled, then turned away, and he went past her, following Gainly to the door. Stepping out into the night, he reckoned he'd gotten no closer to finding his brother, but was satisfied he managed to get on another member of the Timm family's bad side.

'Have an enlightening talk with my father, Ladigan?' came voice from the corner of the piazza. Jack Timm stood there, leaning on a column, smoking.

'Can't say we reached an understanding.'

Jack Timm tossed down his cheroot and approached Ladigan.

'You best stay away from here. It isn't part of the game.'

Ladigan suppressed a grin.

'Losing your cool, Jack? Ain't like you, least the man I met earlier today. Maybe the one I saw last night beating a defenseless woman, though...'

Jack Timm looked ready to boil over and Ladigan got a whiff of whiskey on his breath.

'Jack! Get the hell in here!' Solomon Timm's voice cut off anything else Jack Timm might have said. He jolted and a measure of fear jumped into his gray eyes. Ladigan saw then that Jack Timm was afraid of one thing and that was the man who owned this house.

Jack brushed past him, jostling Ladigan's shoulder. Ladigan let a satisfied grin spread over his lips as the door closed, leaving him on the darkened porch.

CHAPTER FIVE

The blow came fast and sharp, delivered by the back of Solomon Timm's hand. Jack took the full brunt of it across his jaw and staggered backwards, landing on a settee near the bay window. He rubbed his jaw, pain ringing through his teeth.

'What the hell do you think you are doing?' Rage reddened Solomon Timm's face and blazed fire in his eyes.

'What do you mean?'

'You've been seein' whores again.'

'No, I–'

Solomon's gray eyes narrowed.

"Less you want me to beat it out of you you best come clean, Jack. Ladigan told me what happened. You know better. The Timm name means something. I told you to stay away from those women.'

Jack struggled to say something but couldn't find the words. Standing in the drawing-room entryway, Cherish Timm peered at him, an unreadable look on her face.

'I was just having fun.' His words came low and faltering.

'Ladigan informs me there's some dead women.'

'Whores kill themselves sometimes. I can't help that. No one misses them.'

'Where'd you get that bandage on your hand, boy? Ain't from a knife you used to cut some girl with, is it?'

Jack averted his eyes.

'Told you, got bit by a horse.'

Solomon glared at his son, as though accusing him of lying.

'I won't tell you again, Jack. Leave the women and booze alone. The Timm name stands for something and I won't risk your smearing it. You have a responsibility to this family. You've always been disgustingly weak, boy. I can't abide that.'

'Yes, sir...' Jack mumbled, jaw still stinging. He could count himself lucky his old man wouldn't go further than a reprimand tonight; likely only his father and step-mother's previous engagement saved him from a beating.

'We'll take this up later, Jack. You best be more contrite when we do.' Solomon Timm strode from the room, Cherish flashing Jack a frown before following.

With the back of his hand, Jack wiped a snake of blood from the corner of his mouth.

'Someday, old man,' he muttered. 'Someday.

As John Ladigan rode the trail back towards town he wondered if his confrontation with Solomon Timm had been just another in a line of mistakes he seemed bent on making since his arrival in Timmervale. He might have only alerted the man, sent him into a defensive posture. Would that posture turn offensive? Things in Timmervale hadn't exactly proved hospitable as it was. It would be worse with both Timms looking to counter him.

But the visit had told him something. Jack and his father were at odds in some way. Ladigan saw the anger in the elder Timm's eyes when Jack's seeing whores was mentioned and Jack had withered the moment his father's yell beckoned him inside. Jack Timm was afraid of his father. But did it go beyond that? And did it involve his brother's disappearance?

Christ on a crutch, he wasn't some Pinkerton detective. He didn't piece together clues to mysteries; he read sign and tracked down bandits who made mistakes and left evidence of their trails. This was different. Tom had vanished without a trace. Ladigan had two telegrams and damn little else.

Had Tom confronted either Timm? Something about Solomon Timm's blustery manner, maybe the flicker of indignation, made Ladigan think the old man was telling the truth when he claimed he hadn't seen Tom. What about Jack Timm? Had he seen Tom? Or was he simply on Ladigan's case because he was peeled over losing Prilla?

He's dead, Ladigan. You best face the facts...

The dark ball of dread knotted tighter in his belly. Christ, he didn't want to think on that. It wasn't true. It couldn't be true. Tom was simply missing and he would find him.

Then why the second telegram?

A puzzle, that. A puzzle that meant at least one person in Timmervale wasn't so all-fired afraid to get involved. But who? And why?

Ladigan shook his head and breathed deeply of the rapidly chilling night air. He forced thoughts of death from his mind, clung to a desperate hope that Tom was alive and it was just a matter of time till he showed up.

A sound interrupted his reverie.

The noise registered more in his senses than his hearing. He tensed, eyes alert, scanning the trail ahead as he slowed his bay. Moonlight sliced through the trees, falling in sharp wedges across the trail. To either side lay dark forest and the sounds of night creatures. Somewhere a distant screech, maybe some sort of mountain cat. The rustle of bushes. Leaves whispering under the persuasion of the breeze.

Yet something *felt* wrong. And instantly he reverted to what he was, a first-rate manhunter, a man whose nerves became as finely sensitive as the strings on a classical cello, vibrating under the stroking touch of danger. That sixth sense was part of him, woven into his nature. He trusted that feeling.

No mistakes this time.

Ahead an offshoot trail cut into the main one. Had anyone asked him to wager, he would have bet the roll of greenbacks in his pocket that side trail led straight to the back of the Timm Mansion.

The noise came again. Horses, at least two, he reckoned, suddenly in motion. Two men guided their mounts from the side trail onto the main throughway. Moonlight chiseled their faces in stark lines. Ladigan recognized them instantly as the men who'd attacked him at camp. The two men who worked for Jack Timm.

Both held rifles across the crook of their elbows.

He reined up as they lifted their Winchesters to level at his chest.

'Get down from there, Ladigan,' Burgis ordered. Was there a quiver in his voice, despite his having the advantage?

'Don't make no moves towards your gun, neither.' Linch ducked his chin at Ladigan's waist.

'What the hell do you want?' Ladigan's voice came steady and challenging.

'We came to make sure you don't take a notion to go visitin' again.' Anger overrode the nervousness in Burgis's voice this time. 'Now git down...' He levered a shell into the

117

chamber. His hand trembled a hair and a jittery man sometimes pulled the trigger by mistake, so Ladigan nodded and slid from the saddle, keeping his hands in plain sight.

Linch climbed down while Burgis kept the rifle trained on Ladigan's chest.

'Take off your gunbelt.' Linch motioned with his rifle. Burgis stepped from the saddle and moved to the left. Ladigan reckoned he might take out one if he made a lunge but too much distance lay between the two to get them both.

He untied the leather thong holding the holster to his thigh, then unbuckled the belt and let it drop.

'Move over there, away from your piece.' Burgis motioned with the rifle.

Ladigan moved closer to the edge of the trail. He could dive into the forest. It was dark, though the moon silvered everything far too much for his liking. They might hit him, they might not. It was a risk, maybe a big one.

The plan became suddenly moot. Linch had angled around Ladigan's horse. He came from behind the big bay and stood directly in back of Ladigan.

'Hands high, cowboy,' Linch said.

Ladigan had just started to comply when

blinding pain exploded in the back of his left leg. Linch had reversed his Winchester and jammed it into the crook of Ladigan's knee. His leg buckled. He might have kept his feet but Burgis leaped forward, reversing his own rifle and slamming the butt straight towards Ladigan's chest.

Ladigan tried to twist left to avoid the blow but the rifle collided with his chest just above his armpit.

Splinters of pain radiated through his chest. He went backwards, slamming into the hardpack like a felled tree. His Stetson flew off, landing in the dirt a few feet away.

The two men converged on him. He struggled to roll out of the way but a boot-heel from Linch buried itself in the side of Ladigan's thigh, spinning him around.

Burgis let out a guffaw, plainly enjoying getting even for the loss of his eye. He charged at Ladigan, drawing back his foot for a sharp kick at Ladigan's head.

The manhunter let instinct and years of experience take over. These men thought him helpless, were being reckless. As Burgis's boot arced towards his face, Ladigan crossed both hands in front of his chest and clamped his attacker's ankle. He twisted. Hard.

Burgis let out a startled yelp and lost his

balance. He crashed down on the hardpack, stunned, air bursting from his lungs.

Ladigan wasted no time surveying the damage. He gritted his teeth against the pain in his leg and forced himself to his feet.

The other man, shocked into inaction by what happened to his partner, recovered and jerked his rifle towards Ladigan.

Ladigan hurled himself into Linch before the attacker could get the rifle leveled. He jerked the trigger reflexively and lead seared Ladigan's neck. It hurt like hell but it was only a graze.

He plowed the man backwards, coming down atop him, an elbow jammed into his windpipe. Linch uttered awful gagging noises and foam flecked his lips. His eyes bulged and he began to thrash like a wildcat, desperately trying to throw Ladigan off.

Ladigan grabbed Linch's rifle barrel and yanked, hurling himself backward in nearly the same movement. He hit the hardpack and rolled, coming to his feet with the rifle five feet away from the gagging Linch.

Burgis jumped to his feet, shaking his head, then swung his own rifle towards Ladigan.

Ladigan jammed a finger against the trigger and let out a sharp yell: 'Don't!'

Burgis stopped short, rifle wavering. The

man let out a bleat of fear that sounded like a scalded woman and dropped the rifle. He stood shaking, while his companion rolled on the ground, choking and moaning.

'Kick it over here,' Ladigan ordered. Burgis complied without hesitation.

Ladigan scooped up the second rifle and motioned for the man to walk over to his companion, who was now recovering from the elbow to his throat, gasping great gulps of air. Linch got shakily to his feet and both stood eyeing Ladigan like men fixated on a hangman's noose.

'Take off your clothes.' Ladigan moved towards his horse. The big bay was well-trained, used to gunfire and would not move until Ladigan told it to.

'All of 'em?' Burgis asked.

'All of 'em.' Ladigan flung the second Winchester deep into the woods. He'd keep the other.

The men removed their clothing until the garments lay in a pile on the trail.

'Walk back to Jack and tell him to send better men next time if he expects to make a real game of it.'

The men eyed each other, appearing none too thrilled with the prospect of returning to their boss empty handed – and naked.

'Now.' Ladigan said the word low, but it carried a note of threat that made both men jolt. They turned and began heading down the trail. The moonlight made them look like unwashed ghosts drifting through a grave-yard. Ladigan fired the rifle into the air and both men came off the trail at least a foot, then lit out in a run towards the Timm mansion.

He tied the spare rifle to his saddle, located his Stetson and set it on his head, then strapped his gunbelt back on. The men's horses had bolted for the side trail at the sound of rifle fire.

Ladigan mounted, with a click of his heels heading back to Timmervale, a pleased smile on his lips as he imagined the look on Jack Timm's face when his men showed up in their birthday suits.

CHAPTER SIX

Ladigan was a damned fool riding out to the Timm place, Prilla told herself, as she gazed out of a window at the darkened street. Standing in the low-lit back room of the doctor's office, her nerves tightened another notch and she let out a disgusted sigh. He'd been gone over an hour already and she reckoned it would be a minor miracle if she ever saw him again.

What the hell did it matter anyway? He was just another man, another in a long line who saw fit to use her, get what they wanted, then leave.

What about what *she* wanted? Now there was a funny notion. She uttered a clipped laugh. Since when had that been a concern? Since when had she even had the right to ask that *her* needs be met? Like the fine folk of Timmervale told her over and over: she was a useless whore. Hell, in a few years she would have been no good even for that. Ladies of the line didn't hold their age well and men wanted the younger, prettier gals. Ladies of the line got addicted to laudanum or belladonna, contracted diseases that drove them insane, or just plain ended up dead. Like those gals at the saloon who got their throats cut.

A few years? Another funny notion. Most had a few years, but not she. She had less than a year, thanks to Jack Timm, goddamn his soul to eternal hellfire. He had ruined her, hadn't he? Ruined her for all men, including John Ladigan.

Hella'mighty, what kind of thought was that? Why would a man like Ladigan want her anyway? He wouldn't even take it for free.

And why did it suddenly matter to her?

'Jesus H.' Her words came out a whisper and she shook her strawberry-blonde head. With another curse she pushed herself away from the window, sick to death of staring out at a dark street like some silly lovesick housewife. She didn't need anyone, especially him. She could damn well take care of herself.

She went to the examination room, then went to the cabinet that held the laudanum. She tried the door. Finding it locked, she spat a curse. Searching the place, she found a heavy iron. A few sharp blows mangled the lock and the door came open. After grabbing the bottle of laudanum, she suddenly had to brace herself against the cabinet, a dizzy spell making the room spin. Christ, she was tired of those. Tired of vomiting and just plain tired of being tired. She gripped her nerves and pushed away from the cabinet, walking as if tipsy to the big chair in the back room. Pain made practically all her parts tender and her jaw ached like the devil. She deserved the relief the bottle would bring. Maybe it would also drown the loneliness and fear.

She uncapped the bottle and took a swig, the mixture of opium and alcohol bitter and burning as it slid down her throat. Warmth blossomed in her belly, but a fleeting concern took her, one she quickly shoved to the back of her mind. No, she couldn't worry about *that* right now. Too much else troubled her mind, most of which came down to worries that Ladigan would not come back. She could go back to being alone, but she had no money and would not be able to work this town again. Wellerville was a few days ride on a fast horse but how long would she be any good there? A few months? Then what?

She sank deeper into the chair, took another sip of the drug, then set the bottle on the table. A spell of nausea ripped through her belly but quickly subsided. Warmth traveled from her belly through her entire body, and her head lolled, the room shimmering. Bright, everything was so bright, and blurred. Then spiraling. Her eyelids flicked shut, overwhelming fatigue saturating her limbs.

Down, down. Sinking down. With shivery images whirling past, times long ago, times not so far past. Nothing good, nothing special, only a life filled with violence and soiling. The stains of sin dulled the brightness, then turned it scarlet and dripping.

Don't touch me! Don't you touch me!

A voice, pleading, begging, bleeding terror. Her mother's voice. The memory rose from black depths of her mind and she shuddered.

Nooooooo!

That's the way terror sounded. One word, drawn out in a shriek that ended in death.

Images coalesced, sharpened. A barn, the scent of old hay and horse dung ... and *him*. He smelled like cheap whiskey and sweat and some stench he'd splashed on himself that reeked like skunk piss. He had come to their small cabin, a place that was as close to heaven as there ever was before ... before that day.

Her childhood home, where she lived with her mother, her pa an unknown man in an unknown town who had ridden straight for purgatory the moment he discovered his whore had become with child.

Her mother, despite her profession, was a decent, strong woman in her way. She raised Prilla to the age of twelve, trying her damnedest to instill in a little girl the morals she herself never possessed. She'd worked her fingers to the bone, providing food and shelter by making dresses for the fine ladies in town, and secretly selling her favors to their husbands. It was sin, but it was salvation.

He hovered over her mother, whose dress was hoisted up to her thin hips. Standing back towards her, he grabbed a Bowie knife from a sheath at his belt. Prilla recollected how white his knuckles went as he clenched the blade, lifting it above his head.

Just a man. A brutal, vicious man, who came for what her mother offered, then took so much more.

The knife in motion. Light angling through the big double barn doors and glinting from the blade.

Her mother begging. Prilla stood watching from behind a support beam, frozen and wide-eyed, unable to stop what was happening.

Unable to help.

The knife came down with a horrible crunching of bone and muscle and blood spattered a gory streak across the floorboards and soaked strands of hay. The knife plunged down five more times but only the first thrust had counted. It was the thrust that destroyed any chance Prilla ever had of a normal upbringing. It was the thrust that killed her mother.

She could have screamed. She could have run and grabbed a pitchfork and plunged it into his goddamned back. She could have saved her mother.

But she'd done nothing.

After the man left, she had collapsed to the floor and cried. Cried for hours, cried until the darkness came. Cried until someone arrived from town to call on her mother and discovered the awful scene.

But no one found her, because she had run, run as fast and far as she could. It didn't take long for her heart to harden. One choice remained for a girl of twelve if she wanted to survive and she had taken it. After all, her mother had taught her survival came from the wages of sin.

A scream escaped her lips, as Prilla startled awake. Her heart pounded in her throat; tears flooded her eyes. She stared, stunned, at the room, for a moment unable to remember where she was or how she got there. All she could see was the blood, the horror, the past. Nausea surged. Climbing shakily to her feet, she stumbled to the wash-basin and heaved most of the laudanum from her belly. The retching felt like someone burying a fist in her stomach.

When it was over, she staggered to the

window and hurled the basin through. She went back to the dresser and sipped at water from the pitcher, then fell on to the bed.

Ladigan...

His name rose in her mind and she drifted, exhaustion overwhelming her. Settling into a daze devoid of images of her past and a promise of the future.

Ladigan's neck was still sore where the bullet had grazed when he reached the livery and attended to his bay, but only a trickle of blood had come from the wound. He would swab it with carbolic when he reached the doc's.

He grabbed both rifles, his own and the one he'd liberated from Timm's man, slung his saddle-bags over a shoulder and made his way back to the sawbones' office. Once inside he went to the back room, stopping in the doorway, a plunging feeling hitting his gut, as he saw Prilla sprawled on the bed, an arm and one leg hanging off. Had Timm sent someone after her? He had seen death before, but the thought of anything happening to the girl caused something inside him to twist.

He leaned the rifles against a wall, then tossed his saddle-bags on to the chair. He went to the bed and put his hand to her wrist. A sigh of relief escaped his lips when he found a strong pulse. She'd passed out and when, glancing to the small table beside the chair, he spotted the laudanum bottle he reckoned he knew why.

He gently lifted her arm on to the bed, then her leg. Drawing the thin blue blanket up to her chest, he gazed at her a moment. Asleep, she looked somehow innocent and softer. The sudden urge to kiss her sleeping lips made him back away.

Jesus, Ladigan, what's gotten into you?

He was a man, that's what the problem was. A man too long without female companionship and little skill with the fair sex. She was a woman, an angel while asleep, a temptress while awake. God could simply mark down Ladigan's sinful thoughts on the list with his score of others.

After attending to the furrow on his neck with carbolic, Ladigan went to the chair and moved his saddle-bags to the floor. Turning the lantern flame lower, he sat and rummaged through his bags, trying to take his mind off more impure thoughts. He pulled out the tintype and gazed at the picture of him and Tom, the dark feeling in his gut twisting and warning him the worst had happened. Then he stuffed the picture back into the bags and tugged out the two telegrams that had brought him here. He scanned both, something he had done a hundred times over: JOHN SOMETHING BIG STOP TIMMERVALE STOP TIMM FAMILY STOP MY BIG BREAK TOM

His brother hadn't made things very clear, but for him to send that sort of message meant he had discovered something important. Tom wasn't an alarmist or one to traffic in rumor. If he made a claim he was damn sure he had something to back it up.

The second was more cryptic: LADIGAN BROTHER MISSING

That note had sent him riding for Timmervale the moment he'd saddled his horse and cobbled together a few supplies. Who had sent it? That was still a mystery.

He shoved the slips back into his saddlebags and located a pocket-watch, fashioned in gold. It glinted with lanternlight as he pulled it free. An inscription ran across its back: *To John, stay true, Tom.*

His eyes blurred with tears he wouldn't allow to flow and he struggled against the emotion tightening his throat. Stay true. He had because Tom had guided him towards that trail. Without that guidance he reckoned he would have lost all sense of justice and wound up killing every man he tracked out of pure unbridled revenge, until that type was no more, or a bullet found his heart.

He slipped the watch back into the saddlebags and closed the flap. Sinking back into the chair, he gave the sleeping form of Prilla a last glance. He wondered what twist of circumstance had made her the way she was, but was too tired to dwell on it. It didn't take him long to fall into a heavy slumber.

Prilla had feigned sleep when Ladigan returned. She'd slept some, mostly in a daze, but had woken a few minutes before hearing him come in. She'd pressed her eyelids shut as his bootfalls came closer to this room, damned if she could have moved anyway. Her limbs felt heavy as lead posts and her head would not have come off the pillow had her life depended on it.

She had felt him lift her arm and leg to the bed with a gentle touch she didn't rightly figure any man capable of, then cover her with the blanket. From somewhere deep within a shiver of utter warmth had risen up and gone through her, and it disgusted her. What call did she have feeling that way? What call did *he* have being nice to her? First he rescued her from Timm, now this? Bastard.

She wasn't certain whether she was more angry at him or at herself for allowing warm feelings, but she suspected it was the latter. She had switched off her feelings years ago; she had no desire to turn them back on now. He would only disappoint her anyway, by being a man, by using her and hurting her in a way she never thought she would be capable of being hurt.

Through slits, she had watched him pull out a tintype, then telegrams, and last of all a gold watch. The damn thing glittered like a chip of heaven. It came to her then, how to escape her feelings before they grew, how to run. That watch would provide her with the money she needed to start elsewhere, at least for a spell.

Guilt pricked her. Guilt? What the hell was the matter with her? She never felt guilt. It was something she refused to allow since the guilt she'd felt at not helping her mother had crawled deep into her soul and rotted there.

She waited, until he turned the lantern low, until the sound of his breathing slowed and grew deeper. Half an hour dragged by. She waited another fifteen minutes and tried to move her arms and legs. At first they refused to respond but after taking deep breaths and managing to roll to her side, she got them working again.

She struggled into a sitting position on the edge of the bed, head whirling. The room gyrated, streaking with moonlight bleeding through the windows and shadow. Drawing a deep breath, she fought to suppress the nausea roiling in her gut, was only partially successful.

It took another half hour before she could stand without falling back to the bed. Taking cautious steps, she strained to be as quiet as possible. She reckoned manhunters slept with one eye open but Ladigan appeared deeply asleep. She prayed he wouldn't awaken. Leaving was hard enough as it was; she couldn't face him if he caught her.

After a few minutes she steadied, though her stomach remained unsettled. Reaching his saddle-bags she eased them from the floor and went for the door, grabbing one of the rifles on the way. Pausing, she looked back at him, a stab of guilt piercing her again. For one horrible moment she swore a tear came into her eye but she blinked it away, denying it was ever truly there. She fought a sudden urge to walk over and kiss him, backing from the room before that desire became a reality.

Stepping out into the night, an alien feeling

welled in her heart, one she had sworn would never again be allowed to soil her soul.

It felt damn close to sorrow.

CHAPTER SEVEN

Dammit all to hell!

Ladigan cursed, and cursed again. He'd woken to find Prilla gone, along with his saddle-bags and one of the rifles.

Morning sun arced through the blinds, falling across the empty bed. He stood in the back room, alternating between bursts of fury and browbeating himself for being stupid enough to trust her in the first place.

He hadn't expected her to just take off on him, not after coming back the other night. He hadn't expected her to steal his belongings, either, though he rightly should have known better.

Another mistake. They were getting to be a damn foul habit. He reckoned he was all the more peeled because he had actually begun to entertain some feeling for the girl. She was contrary and inclined to ride his nerves but she had made things less lonely at a time when his darkest suspicions told him he might be the last Ladigan left in the world.

Fifteen minutes later he realized he still stood there staring stupidly at the empty bed and vacant spot on the floor where he'd left his saddle-bags. He didn't care so much about the rifle – hell, that he'd taken from Timm's man anyway – or the telegrams; he had read them a hundred times over. But the watch ... that meant something to him. It was all he had left of Tom.

Christ, don't think like that. You'll find him. You have to...

She'd also appropriated the last of his supplies. Restocking in this town was going to be a problem, if Jack Timm had anything to say about it. The mood he was in, he had half a notion to walk into the general store, take what he wanted and throw down cash, but he didn't need to give Marshal Pierson a reason to throw him in a cell right now. With a word from Jack Timm the no-good lawdog might be inclined to do just that and Ladigan couldn't afford any more delay in his search for Tom.

How far could she have gotten?

He could go after her, had half a mind to. At least then he could retrieve his belongings. Strange thing was he found himself reluctant to see her again, if she didn't want to stay. Had anyone asked him whether he missed her he would have denied it to his grave. But the feeling was there, haunting and bitter-sweet.

'Dammit to hell!' He threw a small fit, stamping about, hurling the pitcher – which shattered to shards against a wall – kicking the chair, then suddenly stopping when he realized what a fool he must have looked. He was acting like a child, letting conflicting emotions rule his head and that wasn't like him. What the hell?

He jammed his Stetson on his head and grabbed the remaining rifle, then strode to the front door.

As he stepped out into the new day, warmth hit him, doing absolutely nothing to relieve his foul mood. He was peeled and damn well wanted to stay that way.

He made his way down the alley to the back doors of the livery stable. Entering, a plung-ing feeling of dread took him and near in-stantly turned to fury. He let out a blistering string of curses before locating the attendant, who was stuffing down a breakfast of jerky and steaming coffee.

'What're you doin' here?' The attendant jumped up as Ladigan threw open the door, dumping his coffee in his lap. His mouth clamped shut when he saw the look of rage in Ladigan's green eyes.

'Where the *hell's* my horse?' Ladigan already knew but the attendant's confirmation sent fury through him just the same.

'Your woman came in here and took him during the night. I sleep here, in this back room. I woke up when she pounded on the door and let her in. She said she needed the horse saddled and ready to ride.'

'And you just let her take it?' Ladigan's voice rose to an almost shrill pitch.

The attendant twisted his lips into a guilty expression mixed with fear. Ladigan likely reminded him of a rabid dog.

'Why wouldn't I?'

Ladigan conceded he had a point.

'She say where she was going?'

'She didn't say nothin', 'cept goodbye.'

'I'll be likely renting another horse from you later. Won't be a problem with that, will there?' He glared at the man, who gave a rabbitlike nod.

Ladigan strode from the livery, using the front way. He didn't give a damn whether Timm was around to see him. He was too peeled at Prilla at the moment to think straight and a confrontation with Timm might be just what he needed to work off some steam. That damn girl had made a fool of him. The more he thought it over the more it ... *hurt*. Not only had he lost companionship but that big bay was a damn fine horse.

'Dammit to hell...' he muttered, staring at the street. He took a deep breath, trying to calm himself. Another.

He could still go after her, rent a horse and track her down, but he reckoned he could do that at just about any time. At least *that* was in his bailiwick. Finding his vanished brother, with no clues, wasn't, but it was certainly more pressing. He couldn't afford the delay chasing her down. He had to put the girl out of his mind for now and concentrate on Tom.

Gripping his nerves, he decided to focus on the only two things he could think of doing, though he doubted either would prove much help with Timm controlling the flow of information in this town.

The thought just irritated him more than he was already.

The formal dining-room at the Timm mansion was a masterwork of ostentatious elegance. A crystal chandelier hung over a long mahogany table, the edges of which were carved with a leaf-and-vine motif. Great gold draperies adorned bay windows and sunlight arcing through saffron lace panels made everything appear gilded. Fresh flower arrangements in crystal vases decorated the room.

Silver serving-platters with sliced fruit and soft rolls were set out on the table, along with silver tureens that held eggs prepared in various ways. Steaming coffee from silver carafes scented the room and fresh cream filled sterling creamers.

Solomon Timm took his chair at the head of the table, the way he did every morning. Jack Timm waited, at his father's orders, for Cherish to be seated, before sitting himself.

His foul mood had continued upon waking and seeing the smug rubicund features of his father merely served to intensify it. Ladigan had made fools of his men – again – tipping the game two to one in the manhunter's favor. Possibly higher if Jack counted the scolding he'd gotten from his father last night.

His gaze shifted to Cherish, whose face seemed to glow in the sunlight, eyes shining like little golden chips and her sunflower morning dress tightly caressing the bounties God had given her. She was a damn fine-looking woman, he had to give the old man credit for that much at least. He had picked a woman suitable for a man of his station – had that man been twenty years younger, but that was beside the point – and Jack felt a wave of heat below his belt. He could just imagine those luscious breasts and soft thighs...

'Your men develop a peculiar habit of strolling about at night in the altogether?'

The elder Timm's voice tore Jack from his prurient reverie.

'W-What?' Dread welled in his belly.

Solomon lifted a knife and fork and began slicing at a steak on his plate. Gainly had prepared separate meals for each: steak and over-easy eggs for Solomon Timm, biscuits and gravy with sliced ham for Jack, fruit and scrambled eggs for Cherish. The servant stood towards the corner of the room, next to the buffet, hands folded before his waist.

'Your men, they walked in naked.' He shoved a piece of steak into his mouth, a bit of blood from the rare meat dribbling down his chin. Cherish looked down at her plate, cheeks reddening.

Jack's mouth hung open. How did his father know that? He had been away at the time the men returned and Jack thought he had gotten away with at least that part of it. The truth dawning on him, his gaze shifted to the butler, who raised an eyebrow. That stupid snotty old bastard. He was worse than an old hen. One of these days Jack was going to see to him and make it look like an accident.

'I ... don't know what happened...' Jack picked up his fork and stabbed at his ham, praying his father would let it drop but knowing it wasn't goddamn likely.

'Oh, no?' The elder Timm set his fork down and jammed his elbows into the table, steepling his fingers. 'You were seen talking to them when they came in.'

Goddammit. He glanced at the butler again, whose expression remained one of smug condescension.

'They drank too much, were just out skinny-dipping and forgot their clothes.'

Solomon Timm let out a disgusted grunt.

'Come on, Jack, you can do better than that. They might damn well have been drunk but the closest stream is more than a mile away. You mean to tell me they left their clothes and walked all the way back here?'

'That's what they told me.'

'Must have been quite an indulgence for the mosquitoes.' Solomon Timm couldn't have gotten more sarcasm into his voice had he tried. Jack's anger for the butler ratcheted up another notch.

'Solomon, please.' Cherish lifted her gaze, voice soft. 'It's breakfast. Can't we discuss this at a more appropriate time?'

'Shut up, Cherish,' snapped the elder Timm, face going red. 'Goddammit, Jack, you think I'm addled enough to believe your horseflop? You sent those men after Ladigan, didn't you?' His hard eyes drilled Jack and Jack felt himself shrink. He'd never gotten over his father's berating gaze nor his power to reduce him to a quivering boy of ten, and it goaded him. He drew great satisfaction in reigning over other men, breaking their will, but he goddamn didn't like having it happen to him.

'That sonofabitch deserved to be shown he can't just come waltzing on to Timm property without paying a price.' He said it far more meekly than he wanted, but at least he kept his voice from shaking.

'I *allowed* him in here. I wanted to know what he was up to, so I confronted him. I've never believed in sneaking around for answers, Jack. You know better than that.'

'And just what the hell *is* he up to?' Jack's voice rose and he instantly regretted it as fire jumped into his father's eyes.

'Don't you goddamn use that tone with me, boy. You best show respect when you're addressing me. You know what happens when you step out of line.'

Jack recoiled, despite himself. He knew. No matter how much older Solomon was, the man was strong as a bull. He could easily deliver a thorough thrashing, even to a son who was now a grown man. Last time Jack found himself the target of Solomon Timm's ire he had suffered two broken ribs.

Cherish Timm looked pained, kept her head down.

'What does Ladigan want?' Jack asked in a lower tone, wishing he had the balls to pick up a steak knife and thrust it through the old bastard's stone heart.

'He's looking for some fella, probably a wanted man or something. Showed me a drawing. He's no threat to us unless you make him one.'

'He damn well is...' Jack mumbled.

His father cast him a black look.

'What'd you say?'

'Nothing...' Jack whispered, stabbing at his ham again.

Solomon Timm let out a disgusted sigh and returned to his steak, sawing at the meat. A moment later he threw down his silverware.

'Goddamn breakfast's ruined now, anyway,' he muttered. His gaze centered on Jack, who cringed. 'Have those two idiots of yours go to town for supplies. Make damn sure they don't lift a finger against Ladigan. I hear different and there'll be hell to pay. Is that clear?'

'It's clear.' Jack set down his fork, in no mood to eat.

'Gainly!' Solomon Timm's voice snapped out. He stood, eyeing the servant. 'Give Jack the list of the supplies I asked you to make.'

'Yes, sir.' Gainly hurried from the room to fetch the list. Solomon Timm cast Jack a last look of disapproval, shoved his chair back, then strode from the room.

Cherish Timm looked up, an odd smile on her lips.

'Poor Jack, always the little boy... Well, maybe not always...' The smile grew wider, but suddenly vanished as Gainly came back into the room.

Jack stood, glancing first at Cherish, whose head had lowered again, then at Gainly, whom he had half an urge to murder right then and there. He might have if it wouldn't have brought his father back into the room.

He snapped the paper out the servant's proffering hand and let out a disgusted grunt. He left the room, anger eating away at his innards. He wasn't about to let Ladigan alone, not by a long shot. His father didn't know the real reason the manhunter had come to Timmervale, how it posed a danger to their hold on the town and their riches, riches Jack fully intended would be his once his father was gone.

Ladigan represented a danger, all right, a grave danger. But more than that, he represented a challenge Jack Timm's addiction to power would not let him ignore.

Leave him alone?

Not goddamn likely.

The sun beat down on Prilla's bare legs – she had hoisted her skirt to get comfortable in the saddle – making them sting. Her pale skin burned easily and though it caused discomfort, a far more bothersome pain came from inside, from a part of her she would have sworn no longer existed.

She missed that damn manhunter.

How was that possible? How had he awoken such feelings in her? She'd only known him a day or two. True, he had shown her kindness, stood up for her when no one else in that rotten town or her rotten life ever had. He'd even refused to accept her body in payment.

And how had she repaid him?

By stealing his belongings and his horse. By running out in the middle of the night. By leaving him to face the Timms on his own.

What if he had chosen to let Jack Timm carve off her ear that first night? She might be dead; if not, she'd sure as hell be worthless in her trade.

A surge of nausea interrupted her thoughts, bile sour and burning in her throat. She struggled to keep her stomach down but the combination of heat and constant swaying of the bay beneath her were making it an impossible task.

She had to pee again too. Fourth time this morning.

She slowed the bay, a wave of dizzies coming over her. Swallowing at the bile surging into her throat, she prayed she wouldn't throw up all over the horse. With the heat, neither of them would appreciate living with that stench until they reached Wellerville.

Guiding the horse left, she sent it down a gentle slope to the stream flanking the trail. She slid from the saddle, half-hanging on to the horn until she was able to stand on her own. After tethering the horse to a cotton-wood branch, she stumbled helter-skelter to the stream, barely making it before she collapsed to her knees and vomited the jerky she'd eaten from Ladigan's supplies half an hour earlier.

'Goddammnit,' she muttered, as her stomach contracted again and she retched. She knelt for long moments, gasping, pain-racked, exhausted.

God Almighty, what did she think she was doing? Wellerville was more than a one-day trip and the prospect of making camp alone suddenly terrified her. She was no woodsman. Weren't there bears and mountain cats in this forest? She shuddered. She had a Winchester but even so she'd grown soft, complacent with her trade. At least she always had a roof over her head and a mattress. And once she reached Wellerville, what then? That watch would get her enough in greenbacks to set her up for a week or two, but hope was still a scarce commodity. Things just weren't the same now. Being alone wasn't the same.

You just watched, just stood there, didn't help...

An image flashed unbidden in her mind, the image of a little girl standing hidden and helpless in the barn. Watching her mother's murder. Tears filled her eyes.

Ladigan ... you'll let him die, too. You won't help anyone but yourself. You can't help anyone

but yourself. You're good-for-nothing, Prilla.
Ladigan could never care about a woman who
just abandoned him like a scart rabbit.

'No...' she whispered, then another convulsion wracked her belly. When it passed she lay in the soft sand of the stream bank and curled into a fetal position. Sweat streamed down her face and sides. She became conscious of myriad things: birds singing, the water gurgling over rocks, the sun pounding hot on her face. Mosquitoes ravaged her and black flies snipped bites from her neck and arms. Half the time she had no strength to swat them.

Help me...

The image of her mother again, weaker this time, then Ladigan's face, as if the two events were somehow blending into one another. As the knife plunged down, it was the manhunter being murdered, Jack Timm grasping the Bowie. The scene ran red, a blood-river flowing from her past into the present, ruining any possible future.

What had she done? Why had she needed so desperately to run from him?

Because she was afraid. Powerful afraid. Of him. Afraid of what she'd started to feel. Afraid he would reject her the way she deserved, because she was filth and sin-stained and men like John Ladigan wanted proper ladies with button noses and un-soiled secrets.

Damn him to hell.

She pushed herself up to a sitting position, a measure of strength returning as the nausea abated. A black fly landed on her arm and she slapped it to fly hell and muttered, 'Bastard.'

She drew long breaths, shuddering, at last getting herself under control fifteen minutes later. It took another ten minutes before she could get to her feet and steady herself enough to go behind a tree to heed nature's call, annoyed at herself because she suddenly felt embarrassed peeing in front of a damn horse. After, she collected the canteen, went to the stream and filled it, making sure to go upstream from where she had deposited her breakfast.

You can't just leave him to Timm...

Why the hell couldn't she? She hadn't asked him to help her. She hadn't told him to stick his nose in Timm business. She hadn't told him to stick his hand in a barrel filled with rattlers. He was on his own, the damn fool.

Dammit, he'd been nothing but kind to her, though. It wasn't his fault she'd begun to entertain womanly feelings towards him. He'd done nothing to lead her in that direction, made no promises.

A budding flower of guilt suddenly exploded into a great blossom of countless petals, each scarlet with shame.

Dammit, she couldn't let guilt win. She looked out for herself and that was that.

Just like the fine folk of Timmervale, eh, Prilla?

Forcing the thought away, she let out a strangled groan of disgust and went back to the horse, grabbing the saddlebags and tossing them to the ground. She rummaged inside and found another piece of jerky. She devoured it, unable to control the hunger suddenly ravaging her. The nausea of a short time before vanished and she swallowed chunks of the dried meat whole, keeping it down, at least for the time being. Sitting spraddle-legged next to the saddlebags, she noticed the tintype sticking out. She pulled it free, ran her fingertips over Ladigan's face. The threat of tears was back in her eyes. Emotion clutched at her throat.

You really are starting to care for him...

No, Christamighty, no. It was just loneliness and one of those peculiar emotional moments she'd been having lately. That's all.

And the guilt?

Guilt was for the weak. She was not weak, not anymore, not since that day her mother died.

She shoved the tintype back into the bags and fished out the watch. The yellow metal glinted in the sunlight. Gold all right; it would fetch a pretty penny. Her gaze settled on the inscription. The petals of the guilt flower began to drop off.

The watch must have meant a lot to Ladigan. It came from his brother and his brother might be dead.

'Oh, damn...' she whispered, a tear sliding down her cheek. 'Oh, damn...'

Ladigan had checked the sawbones' office again, just because he was idiot enough to think she might change her mind and come back. Of course she had not, and this time instead of anger he felt haunting sadness. He had merely stared at the empty back room, losing track of time for long minutes, before leaving. Thinking on her did no good. She was gone; that was all there was to it. He'd locate her later and get his horse back.

For now, he had more important matters to ponder. Where had his brother gone? With no clues except for the telegrams and the notion of a big story, Ladigan had too few pieces to form a complete picture. The Timms, at least one of them, were part of it, but whether that tied in with Tom's disappearance was another matter. Did Tom's big story have to do with murdered bargirls? That was another mystery. If it did, then Jack Timm was likely the link, to Ladigan's thinking.

He strode across the wide main street, glancing at the marshal's office and not seeing any sign of the man. Folks roamed the boardwalks, their faces expressionless, strides mechanical. Timmervale was a town that had lost its joy. Its population were merely soulless husks living day to day on what handouts the Timms provided, animals caged in a dust-gilded zoo.

He reached the opposite side and headed for the telegraph office, one of two places he'd decided to check on. Stepping inside, he saw a man sitting behind the counter, tapping keys. He continued his task until Ladigan approached, then stopped and looked up.

The man's face turned a whiter shade and a strange expression of recognition jumped into his eyes, though Ladigan felt certain he'd never met the man.

'You know me?'

The man almost winced at the sound of

Ladigan's voice. He shook his head, eyes darting.

'No. No, sir, I'm sure we never met.'

Ladigan pulled the folded paper from his pocket and flipped it open.

'How 'bout this man? You know him?'

The operator swallowed hard, face going whiter.

'No, him neither...'

He was lying. Ladigan was certain of it.

'You the only fella taps out messages?'

The man nodded. 'I own this establishment.'

'Then you've seen this man, I reckon.'

'Can't say I have.' A bit more defiance but still lying. Ladigan was getting damn tired of the Timm influence, which he was certain lay behind this man's memory failure.

'Let me refresh your mind.' He folded the paper and tucked it back into his pocket. His gaze locked with the operator's. 'A man sent a telegram from this office. That man was the fella in this picture, my brother. Told me about something likely involving the Timms. You know *them*, don't you?'

'Y-yes, I know them. They own the title on this building.'

Ladigan nodded. 'Don't surprise me. Another telegram went out. It told me my

154

brother had gone missing. I want to know who sent it.'

The man shook his head too fast, as if he'd anticipated the question.

'Don't know a thing about it.'

'Why do I get the notion you're not being truthful? That telegram came from this office. We both know it.' His voice lowered a notch, accusation a slow fire in his tone.

'Please, I got two kids and a wife depending on me. I never seen your brother and I don't know nothing about no message.'

Ladigan held the man's gaze, studying him. Had the man been some hardcase he'd cornered he'd consider beating a confession out of him, but the situation was a bit more dicey with this man. If he assaulted him the marshal would have good reason to throw him in a cell, press charges. A town with a Timm judge and jury could hold him long enough to seriously delay his search for his brother. Delay it to a point where if Tom wasn't dead already he would certainly be by the time Ladigan got free.

Besides, this man was no hardcase and he was frightened. He wasn't lying because of some malicious ulterior motive and he was the type Ladigan had taken an oath to protect, not molest. He wasn't certain desperation wouldn't get the best of his temper, though. This man must have seen Tom and whoever sent the second telegram.

Ladigan sighed. He'd let the man off the hook for now, but not for long.

'Next time I come back here I'll expect better answers. Think it over.' Ladigan's hand touched the butt of his Peacemaker, his meaning clear, and the rest of the blood drained from the telegraph man's features.

Ladigan left the office, slamming the door behind him.

Outside he paused, frustration growing stronger. He hoped the second place on his list provided better results.

He started down the boardwalk, gaze scanning the passersby for any sign of Jack Timm or his two useless sidekicks, but they were nowhere to be seen.

Three blocks clown, he reached the newspaper office, the Timmervale *Gazette*, and entered. Once inside, the pungent scent of ink assailed his nostrils and the clatter of a press assaulted his ears. He glanced around at the machinery and tables holding spread-out rolls of paper, eventually spotting a small man with a barrel chest and graying hair poised over wooden letters, arranging them into a headline. A second man, scrawny and younger with rolled-up sleeves, operated the press but Ladigan targeted the older man as the owner.

He came up behind the man, who with all the noise hadn't heard him enter. The man jolted when Ladigan flipped open the drawing of his brother in front of his face.

The man turned, and for the briefest of moments shock lassoed his features. Ladigan also noticed something else, half the man's jaw was not right, as if it had been recently broken. Same with his nose, which was slightly swollen and crooked. He stared at the paper, then at Ladigan, recovering enough to get his poise back. He signaled to the man running the press to shut down. The resulting silence left Ladigan's ears thrumming.

'You know this man?' Ladigan asked, tone demanding.

'Why should I?' Another scared man, though this one covered it better. Only the slightest of breaks in his voice said he was lying.

'This is my brother. He was writing a story. I figure one of the first places he might stop when he came to Timmervale would the newspaper office.'

The man blinked, frowned.

'He might have stopped by once or twice.'

A surge of relief washed over him. Maybe he would get a lead to Tom at last.

'What did he say when he was here?'

The man shrugged.

'He was seeing if I needed any reporters, said he might have a story for me, if I was interested.'

'You give him an answer?'

The man drew a breath, his composure solidifying.

'Told him I had enough reporters and couldn't help him.'

'He say anything else?'

'No, nothing.'

'You seen him since?'

The man's eyelids fluttered.

'No, haven't seen him. I figured he left town and went to look for a job elsewhere.'

Ladigan felt certain the story had more to it, things the newspaper man deliberately left out. But he got the notion the man was telling the truth when he said he hadn't seen Tom recently.

'What happened to your face?' Ladigan ducked his chin at the man's jaw.

The man's hand drifted to his jaw, and fear came into his eyes again.

'Fell off a horse a few weeks back.'

'You best ride more carefully.' His tone

said he didn't believe a word of it and the newspaper man averted his gaze.

'Reckon, I will...' His voice was almost a whisper, then after a long pause he added, 'Your brother, I hope you find him.'

'Do you?'

The man frowned. 'I do, Mr Ladigan. I sincerely do.'

Ladigan nodded, not surprised for a minute the man knew who he was without Ladigan's having told him. Likely the horse he'd fallen off of was named Timm.

The newspaperman wasn't telling all he knew, but Ladigan would come back to him. He figured the telegraph man was an easier break.

For now, he couldn't help feeling out of his element with detective work and damn near out of options where finding Tom was concerned. All those years growing up, his brother had never let him down; John Ladigan wished to hell he could claim the same.

He went to the door, pausing with his hand on the handle. He looked back to the newspaper man, who was staring at him with a peculiar look Ladigan couldn't read.

'You ever lose someone you care about, Mr...?'

'Mortimer, Jim Mortimer.'

'Mr Mortimer. It's a hell of a feeling.'

The man bowed his head, then looked up again.

'Mr Ladigan...'

'Yeah?'

'Nothing ... nothing at all.' The newspaper man turned and went back to arranging letters.

Outside on the boardwalk, Ladigan heard the press start clattering and shook his head. He gotten little more than he already knew. Tom had been here, and gone. Someone had seen him. Then nothing.

His hand balled into a fist, and he wished he could hit something, anyone, preferably someone with the Timm name attached to his no-good hide.

He walked down the boardwalk, the late morning sun baking the street and raising shimmering waves of heat. A passing buckboard swirled clouds of stifling dust. A moment later he stopped before the dress shop and she was back in his mind again. He'd promised her a new dress, hadn't he? A blue gingham in the store window looked about her size, but what the hell did he know about such things?

She ain't coming back. What use would it be?

Well, eventually he would track her and

retrieve his horse, if not his pride. She'd likely need something nice to wear when he brought her in for horse-stealing.

He almost laughed at the thought, knowing damn well he'd let her go and likely hand her enough greenbacks to set up temporarily before he left. He *was* a damned fool, after all. She'd told him so, and now he could believe it.

He was also a man who kept his promises. He went into the dress shop and a woman approached him, raking him up and down with an appreciative gaze. Although she spotted him a good fifteen years, she was apparently widowed and ready not to stay that way.

'Dress in the window, the blue one, how much?' He fully expected her to refuse to sell it to him on Timm's orders, but she merely looked disappointed.

'That's fine as they come.' Her gaze got more familiar with him and he got more uncomfortable. 'Fifteen dollars, wrapped.'

He brought out his roll of greenbacks and peeled off the bills. She plucked them from his hand. It dawned on him that Jack Timm would have anticipated the hotel, saloon and other shops Ladigan might patronize, but a dress shop hadn't occurred to him.

The owner could not have been in the crowd that first night he rode in, either.

She wrapped the dress and handed it to him, her gaze back where it shouldn't be. He tipped his finger to his hat and left, feeling somehow dirtier than two weeks on the trail had ever made him.

He left the wrapped dress on the bed in the back room of the sawbones' place, then went to the livery and rented a horse.

Riding out to the campsite he'd formerly occupied, he tethered the horse to a tree. He had little desire to stay in the empty room now and needed time to think, figure out some sort of strategy for finding his brother. He stared out at the stream, unable to come up with the answers he hoped for. His only two leads had an aversion to the truth, but he doubted either could provide a solid trail to Tom's whereabouts. He'd spent years tracking men successfully, but when it counted most he couldn't live up to the legend in that pulp novel.

Frustration surged back, and with it a sense of hopelessness. Lowering himself to the ground facing the water, he buried his face in his hands. Lost in his thoughts, he didn't stir for a very long time.

CHAPTER EIGHT

Burgis stepped from the general store, arms loaded with supplies Jack Timm had told him to fetch for Solomon Timm. From what he gathered old Solomon had spotted them coming back in their altogether last night and was south of happy about it. Jack was none too pleased they'd been seen either. He'd promised dire consequences for that screw-up. Burgis felt a stitch in his gut at that prospect. He'd be lucky if he didn't lose his other eye.

He let out a curse at that no good sonofabitch Ladigan and spat on the boardwalk. Linch had gone to see if the lawdog had seen any signs of Ladigan in town today, so they could report back to Jack. They'd been ordered not to touch the manhunter, a directive that pleased him more than he dared admit. He had no desire to take a third whuppin' at the manhunter's hand. Way Burgis saw it, they'd probably been lucky to get away with just the dignity kicked out of them last night.

That didn't mean if he got the chance to backshoot the manhunter he wouldn't take it. But for now he had to concentrate on getting back on Jack's good side, 'fore the younger Timm made Ladigan's beating look like youngins' rough housin'. He'd seen Jack torture critters to death a few times, take a great glee in hearing the pitiful sounds they made as he burned their flesh or skinned them alive – slowly. Burgis considered himself a tough character; he had no qualms 'bout killin' a fella who got on his bad side. But when it came to inflicting pain and taking sick pleasure in watching things die, Jack Timm made him look like an amateur. He'd fought tough men, but both Timm and Ladigan made him break out in a nervous sweat.

Burgis shuddered, thinking again about what Jack might do to him and Linch once the rage he was bottling up over their failure was let loose. He considered taking the buckboard and heading out of town but Jack would only catch up to him eventually. Then he'd be the one skinned alive. Slowly.

He stepped off the boardwalk and set the packages in the back of the buckboard. Lifting his hat, he wiped sweat and grime away from his forehead and adjusted his patch, then peered down the street. He glanced at the faces of folks going about their day to day business, each looking strangely humorless. Sorry bastards, all of 'em, he reckoned, but he didn't care. Least they weren't on the receiving end of Jack Timm's fists.

He started across the street, intending to go fetch his partner, when he stopped dead, his one eye catching a sight that brought a sadistic smile to his face. He watched for a moment, the smile widening, growing meaner.

The door to the marshal's office opened and Linch stepped out. He spotted his partner and headed over to him.

'What the hell you gawkin' at?' Linch jammed a rolled cigarette into his mouth, then fished a lucifer from his pocket and lit up.

Burgis ducked his chin towards the side street leading to the sawbones' office and the cigarette nearly dropped out of Linch's mouth.

'Hot damn, that's...'

Burgis nodded. 'Sure as hell is. That's our ticket for gettin' on Jack's good side when we get back.'

Linch plucked the cigarette from his mouth and let out a low whistle.

'Should we just bring her back with us?'

'Hell, no! Bad enough Ladigan kicked our

britches. Don't need some girl doin' it.'

'Brave man.' Linch eyed his partner with disgust.

'You do it, then. And if she gets away or Ladigan comes along you can be the one who goes crawlin' to Jack and tells him what happened. Again.'

Linch's expression went somber.

'Reckon I see your point.'

'She went into the sawbones' office. They must be hidin' out there since the hotel won't take 'em.'

'Let's get a look in the window and make sure Ladigan ain't there, too.'

Neither moved for a moment, each thinking over the suggestion and not particularly wanting to be the one who went first.

'We best do it now, 'fore she gets away.' Burgis moved towards the side street. They scuttled along, close to the buildings, coming up beside a window. Linch peered inside, then went to the next window and did the same.

'Ladigan ain't there. Maybe he stayed at his camp.'

Burgis eyed him. 'Why would he just let her alone after savin' her?'

Linch shrugged. 'She's just a whore. Reckon he done used her and told her to git.'

Burgis thought that sounded like a reasonable explanation and that made things a doubly good prospect.

They slipped from the alleyway and hurried back to the buckboard, climbing into the seat. Burgis took the reins, the relief he felt almost making him giddy. He let out a nervous titter and headed back to the Timm mansion.

Prilla closed the door and pressed her back against it, drawing a deep breath. She'd left the horse with the livery attendant and hauled the saddle-bags and rifle back with her, the short walk after the long ride feeling like a hundred-mile trek. She prayed she hadn't been spotted coming back to the sawbones' office, but in this town, with everyone a Timm look-out, she figured word would get back soon enough. It was still daylight after all, though already the shadows were lengthening and the sun would soon disappear behind the blue Rockies.

She pushed herself away from the door, legs shaking from nerves, as well as fatigue. What if Ladigan didn't want her back here and threw her out into the street? She would deserve it, but then she would have nothing, no watch to hock, no money, and no chance of living long enough to...

No, she couldn't let herself back out now. For once in her life she had to face up to something. He deserved at least an explanation. Then he could do with her what he would. Her mother had survived on her own and raised a child, at least to the age of twelve; she would survive too. Somehow.

She braced the rifle against the wall and walked towards the back, expecting to hear sounds of him there, but when none came she wondered if he hadn't just deserted the place. Maybe he had found his brother and gone back to where he came from. What reason would he have to stick around Timmervale otherwise? Certainly not the prospect that she might change her mind and come crawling back.

She hauled the saddle-bags to the back room and tossed them on the chair, her whole body shaking now and nerves fluttering deep in her belly.

Ladigan wasn't here but a brown paper-wrapped package lay on the bed. She peered at it for long moments, heart thumping in her throat. The gloom deepened in the room by the time she eventually moved. Going to the bed, she sat on the edge of the mattress, placing the package on her lap and running her fingers over the paper. Untying the string, she pulled back the paper. Blue material peeked out and her breath clutched.

A dress. A gingham dress. Blue, her favorite color. Something soft and innocent-looking, something only a decent woman would wear, not a whore.

He promised you a dress...

Ladigan was a man of his word. Who would have ever thought any man could keep a promise made when they weren't getting something in return?

Her eyes misted over and a tear slipped down her cheek.

She held the dress up before her, then laid it out on the bed and dried her eyes with the corner of the blanket. If she put on the dress maybe when he came back he'd see her in it and there'd be a chance...

No, no chance. What was she thinkin'? He was just living up to his word and there was nothing more to it than that. Nothing more at all.

A knock sounded and she jolted, looking up. Ladigan was back and it was time to face him and accept responsibility. She would stand there and take anything he dished out, no matter how much it hurt.

He's not like the rest...

Wasn't he? He was a man and a man didn't know what went on inside a woman, how words could wound even a hard woman such as herself, one who had stupidly let her guard down.

She stood, forcing herself to walk through the examination room to the front. Five feet from the door, she stopped, as sudden dread made her stomach drop.

Why?

Because Ladigan wouldn't knock, would he? He would just come right in. He had no reason to knock because he would not expect her to be here.

Someone else stood behind that door. Had someone seen her ride in?

She stared at the door, heart starting to pound faster. A bead of sweat trickled down the side of her face.

It's him. You know it's him. He's toying with you by knocking...

Don't be foolish, she told herself. He wouldn't dare come here with Ladigan around.

Unless he knows Ladigan's gone...

The door handle started to turn. Dammit, she hadn't bothered to bolt the door.

She fought to move but her feet felt frozen to the spot. Shivery fear went through her belly like snakes sliding over each other.

The door swung open and she let out a sharp gasp.

A man stood in the doorway, the creeping dusk making him look like a dark devil come a-callin' for her soul.

'Well, hello there, Prilla,' the man said in a flat tone. The oily smile was on his face and his cold gray eyes glittered with a violent promise to finish what he started the other night.

'J-Jack...' Had she actually spoken? The roar of her blood pulsing in her ears made her unsure. She forced herself to breathe.

'Come with me, Prilla. We have unfinished business.' He held out his hand, palm up. In his other hand, a Bowie knife, his knuckles bleached from squeezing the handle so tightly.

Her gaze flashed to the rifle leaning against the wall. She saw no chance getting to it before he was on her and cutting into her flesh.

Jack Timm caught her intent, took a step sideways to get between her and the rifle.

'Don't make this harder on yourself, Prilla. Our business won't take long and life can go back to normal after that. I promise.'

'You bastard...' she said through clenched teeth.

'You're just noticing?' He stepped over to her and grabbed her arm, dragging her out into the dying day.

John Ladigan stood after sitting by the stream for hours, mood no better than when he'd come to this spot. His brother was still missing, Prilla was still gone and his whole life had turned straight to horse-dung.

With nothing more to go on than a tenuous link to the Timms, he'd come to the resolution the telegraph man and newspaper owner were going to tell all they knew and tell it soon, no matter what method it took to get it out of them. Sitting here feeling sorry for himself was no help. This thing needed finishing, and he needed the truth, even if he was goddamn afraid to face it.

He reckoned some folks might have got a laugh out of the famous John Ladigan being afraid of anything. An avenger, a legend in the making. That sort of man didn't fear. That sort of man had icewater in his veins and steel in his nerves. The pulp novels said as much.

But they were wrong. Only a stupid man didn't fear. And only a coward refused to admit it.

He was afraid, more so than he'd ever

been. Afraid the answer he sought would lead to the loss of his brother That dark feeling inside was telling him something he wanted to deny with every ounce of his being. He was afraid Tom was dead. He was also afraid he had feelings for a woman who had robbed him and left him smack in a hornet's nest called Timmervale.

A wise man feared. A weak man controlled. A fool denied.

Only the future would tell which label fit a man named John Ladigan.

He mounted and heeled his rented horse, a strawberry roan, towards town. Dusk swooped in, shadows stretching across the trail, shifting under the breeze like clutching talons. A chill began to move through the air. The dread inside his belly strengthened.

By the time he reached town the sun dropped behind the distant mountains and hanging lanterns glowed in front of shops.

He rode straight to the livery, the front way, and the attendant gave him a puzzled look Ladigan couldn't read immediately. Then he saw his big bay safe in a stall and something inside him wanted to jump for joy.

'Your woman came back, Ladigan,' the attendant said, taking the reins to the roan while Ladigan went to his horse and stroked the bay's nose.

'When?' Ladigan moved away from the stall.

'Short while ago. She looked a bit sick but none the worse for wear.'

'She say where she was going?'

The man shook his head.

Ladigan nodded and went out the back way. He had intended to head directly to the telegraph office, but Prilla's return had changed things. He wondered why she'd come back and what he was going to say when he saw her. Part of him wanted to let her have it in no uncertain terms while the other part...

The other part wanted to tell her he was glad she'd come back and more glad she'd returned his horse.

He almost smiled at the thought of the expression that would bring.

A moment later his manhunter's intuition went off like a swindled tinhorn. The office door hung open, the interior gloomy in the dusk, forbidding. His hand went to the butt of his Peacemaker as he stepped inside, senses alert. The time for mistakes was over.

He saw the rifle leaning against the wall, found his saddle-bags in the back room, but no sign of the girl. He went back to the front room and closed the door, then lit the lanterns in the front and back rooms. He noticed the dress set out on the bed. She had been here, not long ago. Where was she now? Why had she left again?

Maybe she had just come back to return his belongings and the spread-out dress was telling him she had no interest in facing up to him after running off.

His manhunter's sixth sense put a quick denial to that theory, told him the reason was something far darker. He saw no signs of a struggle, but could someone have seen her ride in and interrupted whatever she planned?

Jack Timm...

If she hadn't left under her own power, Jack Timm was the number one suspect. The only suspect. He enjoyed playing cat and mouse with Ladigan, but with Prilla ... with Prilla his sole aim would be revenge.

'Dammit,' he said under his breath and headed to the door. He left the office, headed up the side street and onto the boardwalk. Upon reaching the marshal's office he threw open the door, his nerves tight and anger unreined now that the girl might be in danger.

Marshal Pierson sat behind his desk,

scooping beans into his mouth from a tin bowl. The man started, gaze locking on Ladigan.

'What the hell you doin' back here?' Bean-broth dripped from his chin. He set his fork in the plate and dabbed at the drippings with a bandanna.

'Decided it was time I started getting some answers, Marshal.'

'Think I done told you this town was Timm Territory.'

Ladigan's temper got the best of him then. Three steps took him to the desk. Grabbing a fistful of the lawdog's shirt he hauled him half-out of his seat.

'Goddammit, Ladigan, I'll have you in a cell for this,' the marshal sputtered, spittle collecting at the corners of his mouth, but fear jumped into his eyes.

'You listen good, because I'm goddamn running out of patience with this town and the lot of you acting like whipped curs. You seen Prilla at any point today?'

'P-Prilla...?' The man made fish movements with his mouth.

'She came in maybe a bit over an hour ago. She ain't where she's s'posed to be.'

'I ain't seen her, Ladigan, I swear. I thought she was with you.'

Ladigan judged the man was too scared to lie and decided on another tactic.

'The man in that drawing I showed you ... you got five seconds to tell me anything you know about him 'fore I decide you look better with a third eye.'

The man's eyes widened and his voice climbed higher in pitch.

'Goddammit, Ladigan you can't be serious!'

'Test me.' His tone gave the marshal his answer.

The man hesitated, swallowing hard.

'I-I can't...'

'One.' Ladigan twisted the man's shirt a bit more.

'Ladigan, please, you don't know how Jack Timm can be.'

'I don't give a damn. Two.'

'He might kill me.' The man was close to tears and Ladigan had his gun suddenly in his free hand, the barrel jammed to Pierson's forehead.

'Three. You're a goddamn pathetic excuse for a lawman, Pierson. You would have let that monster carve off a girl's ear and not lifted a finger.'

'I was being merciful. He would have done far worse if anyone stepped in.'

'Four. I can't see how. You want to let me get to five?'

The marshal swallowed again, sweat streaming down his face now. Ladigan skritched back the hammer. Slowly.

'All right, all right, like I told you in the first place I seen that man in your drawing.'

'Tell me and be quick about it.' He didn't remove the gun.

'He came in here for a few days, 'bout three weeks back. Said he was writing some sort of story and stayed at the hotel a couple days. That's the last I saw of him.'

Ladigan's gaze narrowed. 'What else?'

'That's it, I swear, Ladigan. Jesus, I swear.'

A dark stain appeared on the front of the man's trousers.

'You piss yourself every time Jack Timm comes to call too?'

Pierson didn't answer, but his face went red.

'I'm gonna be having the same talk I had here with a couple others in this town. You won't lift a finger to stop me or move on me afterward, that clear?'

The marshal nodded. Ladigan pulled the Peacemaker away, eased the hammer back and holstered the gun. He thrust the marshal back into his chair and backed away. He hadn't gained much but sure as hell felt better.

He had no doubt the lawdog wouldn't keep his mouth shut but he reckoned the marshal would be little threat from this point on.

He stepped out into the night, leaving Pierson quaking in his chair.

Jack Timm, one hand clamped about her arm, fingers digging in until pain radiated down to her fingertips, dragged Prilla down the opposite street and through the forest that flanked the east side of Timmervale. The spot lay only half a mile from the sawbones' office, but it might as well have been a hundred. The patch of clearing was secluded, just far enough away so no one would hear her screams. It would not have mattered if they had. Her foolish running had resulted in this predicament. Had she stayed near Ladigan she would not be at the mercy of the monster who peered at her with that oily smile and breathed old gin into her face.

Moonlight gave his features a skeletal look, dark eyes sunken into bone-white flesh, leering grin spreading over thin lips.

'I'm going to enjoy this, Prilla. Really I am. It will solve everything, you'll see. I can't risk my father knowing. I told you that.'

He jammed her against a tree. Moonlight glinted from the knife in his hand, as he held it before her eyes.

'No ... please, please not that...' She'd rather he killed her than go through with the inhuman thing he planned.

'Don't see why you got such an objection, Prilla. Plenty other gals at the saloon would give Jack Timm whatever he wanted to be on his good side. You were always different, weren't you? You gave it 'cause I paid for it but never gave it 'cause you wanted to play up to me. I reckon that's what made you my favorite, least for a while. That's what made you a challenge. But I've grown tired of it, Prilla. And I can't have you ruining things for me with my father, can I? It's better this way.'

He was not going to let her live. She saw it in his eyes right then. He was going to do that awful thing while she was alive to make her suffer, then kill her. He wanted her to watch every drop of blood that spilled from her body and agonize with every tear that flowed from her heart.

'I'm sorry...' she whispered, lips quivering, tears streaking from her eyes. She didn't mean it for Jack Timm but he grinned wider and it gave her a desperate idea.

'Now that's more like it, Prilla.'

'I-I'm sorry, Jack. I truly am.' She struggled to keep her voice steady. 'I know I was your favorite. I still wanna be. I'll do what you want. I'll be nice to you.' Choking back disgust, she pushed against him, running her hands over his vest and trying to press her quivering lips to his.

He thrust her back and her head collided with the tree, sending sparks of light before her eyes and a ringing pain through her skull.

'You stupid bitch. You think it's that easy? You think I wouldn't know what you were up to?' He spat at her; saliva dripped down her cheek. 'I'll have you first, don't you worry none. I don't give a damn whether you're nice or fighting like a wildcat. Fact I might prefer the latter. But you ain't smart enough or slick enough to fool ol' Jack.'

He pressed the knife-tip to the top of her blouse, plucking at the cloth and easing it down over her shoulder. A few more inches and he would expose her breast and God knew what he would do with the blade then.

Terror made her head reel and she struggled to keep it clear because if she collapsed it would be too easy for him. If he was going to kill her she was going to take her toll on his hide first.

She screamed, a short choppy thing, as her

hand came up and her nails raked his face. He let out a yelp and his free hand went to his face, blood dripping between his fingers.

'Goddammit, woman–' he started, but she didn't let him set himself again. She hoisted her knee and buried it in his groin. A burst of air exploded from his lungs. The knife at her shoulder broke her skin as his hand jerked, but it was only a surface cut. Blood trickled from the wound.

Jack Timm stood frozen, spittle bubbling from his lips, eyes wide and blazing with pain and fury. He leaned over suddenly and retched. She brought her knee up again, this time into his face.

It connected with a muted *crack* and he collapsed to the ground, curling into a ball. She stared for a second, considering grabbing the knife from his hand and plunging it deep into his black heart. But the memory of the man stabbing her mother brought a gout of nausea to her belly and she turned and fled.

'I'll get you, Prilla, goddammit I will!' She heard him yell behind her, his voice spurring her on. Hot gasping breaths tore at her throat and her legs felt drained of all strength, but she wouldn't allow herself to stop. He would soon recover and come after her again.

The muscles in her legs began to fail. She

stumbled, righted herself, stumbled again. Only a few hundred feet to go before she hit a street leading into town. So close, so close...

Her heart threatened to crash from her chest. Muscles quivering. Pain, so much pain, in her legs, her lungs, her chest.

Hardpack beneath her feet and relief gave her a burst of adrenaline. She had made it. She ran up a side street onto the main throughway. If she could just make the sawbones' office and get the rifle...

God, Ladigan, please be there, please–

The marshal's door opened and she saw Ladigan step out onto the boardwalk. She let out a cry and he came towards her. She was barely conscious of collapsing into his arms.

The next thing she knew they were back in the front room of the doc's. He had placed her on the small sofa and was peering at her. The cut on her shoulder was bandaged. She trembled all over and, drawing deep breaths, fought to regain her composure. She felt sick again.

'What happened?' Ladigan's voice, soothing, solid, softer than usual, comforting beyond anything she had ever heard.

'Jack ... Jack Timm. He came here and took me into the woods. He was going to kill me, worse...'

'Worse?'

She looked at him, shook her head, unable to tell him what Timm had planned. She saw his face redden, pure anger raging in his green eyes.

'He ain't likely to come back here, but if he does...' Ladigan stood and fetched the rifle from the wall, handing it to her. 'Kill him. Don't hesitate, just shoot.'

'Where you goin'?' She didn't want him to leave her, in fact, she was damn terrified of being alone.

'I'm riding out to the Timm place. I got a notion Timm's father don't know half of what his son's been up to. I also got a notion Jack knows something about my brother. He's gonna come clean with it. After I see him, he won't be in any shape to ever hurt you again. I promise you that, Prilla.'

'You're a man of your word, Ladigan. I reckon I know that now. But you can't just kill him in cold blood, not in Timmervale.'

'Don't intend to unless he draws on me. But I'll bring him to the territorial marshal and tell what's been happening in this town. Jack Timm will hang one way or the other.'

Her eyes turned pleading, glassy with tears.

'They won't take your word. Timms are too powerful.'

'It's a long trip...' An ominous note hung in his tone.

'I'm going with you. You can't leave me alone.'

'No, stay here. I don't need you gettin' in the way. You ain't in shape to ride right now, anyway.'

She was about to object but saw it would do no good. Something had changed about him. He had focus now.

He headed for the door, giving her a last look, a grim expression. Something else shone in that look, something that told her he was relieved she was back and still alive and that he cared.

Ladigan opened the door and a dark figure stood on the threshold. She swore the manhunter's hand blurred as it flashed to his gun and whipped it level.

CHAPTER NINE

'If you intend to shoot me, Mr Ladigan, I suggest you get it over with.' The man in the doorway didn't flinch and held Ladigan's gaze.

'You best have a reason for sneaking around outside the door, Mr Mortimer. In light of what just happened to Prilla, it best be a damn good one, too.'

The newspaperman's gaze shifted to the woman sitting on the sofa then back to Ladigan.

'I saw you in the street and followed you back here.' Mortimer's voice remained steady. 'If you lower the gun, I'll tell you the rest.'

Ladigan studied the man, hearing sincerity in his tone and deciding he wasn't likely a threat. He lowered the gun and holstered it, but remained on the alert.

'Make it quick.' Ladigan motioned the man inside, then closed the door.

The newspaperman doffed his derby hat and eyed Prilla.

'I'm sorry I didn't help you the other night, ma'am. Of all people I should have done better, and I'm rightly ashamed.'

Prilla's lips drew tight.

'It's what I expect from this town. Jack Timm puts the fear of God in everyone living here.'

'Ain't the fear of God, ma'am. Fear of God's what brought me here, that and something else.'

'Say what you came to say, Mr Mortimer.' Ladigan folded his arms.

The newspaper man shifted feet, cleared his throat.

'I knew your brother better than I let on. He came to offer me the biggest story this town, maybe the Territory's ever seen.'

'About the Timms?'

''Bout one of 'em anyway, but it would have repercussions for the whole clan. Your brother saw what the Timms had done to this town, how their money takes care of folks but also keeps them caged. Jack Timm mostly. His pa ain't much better, though he don't come here. He lets Jack do what he wants, long as it don't affect the family name.'

Ladigan frowned.

'That what Solomon Timm cares about, the name?'

Mortimer nodded.

'That and that pretty young second wife of his.'

'Figured she must not be Jack's real mother.'

'No, his real mother passed on from the consumption four years back.'

'I met Cherish Timm. I reckon the old man must have some of the same habits as his son.'

Mortimer cocked an eyebrow.

'What do you mean by that?'

'Saw bruises on her jaw. Same type Prilla's got. Figure the old man handed down a family trait to his son.'

The newspaperman looked perplexed, shook his head.

'No, no, I don't see how that can be. Everybody knows the old man treats that gal like a flower. He's sharp with her, don't take no back-talk and keeps her in her place. But I doubt he'd lift a hand to her. He saves that for his son. Beats the hell of Jack even now the kid's grown. Always has. Reckon that's what made Jack such a bastard.'

The news surprised Ladigan but he had to wonder if the newspaper man weren't mistaken. Someone had hit the woman.

'What about you, Mr Mortimer? Still stickin' to that horse story?'

A humorless smile turned the news-paperman's lips.

'No, Jack Timm broke my nose and gave me these bruises. He wanted to know what your brother told me, but I convinced him I knew nothing. I can take a lot of pain.'

'What else you know about my brother, Mr Mortimer?'

'Like I said, he offered me a story but

didn't give me all the details. He thought it would be enough of a disgrace to ruin the Timms's hold on the town. As a token of good faith he told me a young'in was involved, and that something had happened to Cherish. He believed she was raped one night when the old man was out, and that Solomon Timm covered it up. But there's more to it than that, least your brother said so. He wanted me to agree to print the story, hit the Timms in their own backyard.'

'Did you agree to print it?'

'I told him before I'd print something like that I needed proof that what he was telling me was the God's honest. He told me he planned to get into the Timm place and find some kind of evidence to go with what he already had. He figured there was a paper trail locked in Timm's safe leading to a foundling home in St Louis.'

'I don't quite see how that amounts to a big enough scandal to destroy a family as power-ful as the Timms, Mr Mortimer. The old man's got enough money to hire a battery of fancy-frocked East coast lawyers and men to attend to damage control, though it might put a few nicks in the gold plate.'

'Your brother seemed certain of it, Mr Ladigan. From the short time I knew him

189

he impressed me as the type to be positive of something that big before he made a move against a family as powerful as the Timms.'

'I'm inclined to agree, but there's missing pieces. Maybe I best look for those pieces myself.'

'Your brother said the same thing before he ... disappeared.'

Ladigan's belly tightened.

'You didn't see him again after that?'

Mortimer shook his head.

'He might as well have walked into the thin air. I didn't think much of it for a few days, then I got to worryin'. He was s'posed to check in with me on the following Friday but I never saw him again.'

'The telegram I got...'

'I sent it, with the help of the telegraph man. It took some convincin' to get him to risk it, but he hates the Timms.'

'Thought they owned his place?'

'They do, and they hold that over him, make him do whatever they want. He used to own a farm near where the Timm mansion ended up. They had the bank man foreclose on his loan and took the land from him. The shop was Solomon's gesture of "good will".'

Ladigan nodded, the muscles at either cheek quivering with tension.

'Jack Timm a killer, in your estimation, Mr Mortimer?'

The newspaperman bowed his head, as if thinking it over, then looked up.

'He's a cruel, brutal man. I wouldn't put it beyond him, not by a long shot, but if you're asking did he kill Tom, I can't tell you for sure.'

'He would have killed me tonight,' said Prilla, spite in her tone. 'I saw it in his eyes.'

'You reckon he might have killed those saloon girls?' Ladigan asked Mortimer.

'Word is they killed themselves, but word also is Jack was with all them women before they died. But he was seen leaving them alive, so can't say he did it.'

'Why not kill Prilla, then?'

'If he killed the others, you mean? Makes it look funny, don't it? But Jack usually made no effort to hide who he's been with during his forays into town. But I never heard of him being with you, ma'am.' Mr Mortimer's gaze cut to Prilla.

'Jack told me I was his favorite, said he wanted to keep things quiet 'tween us so the other gals wouldn't get to talkin'. I'm sure they did anyway, but I don't have the habits some of them did, with laudanum and gin, I mean. Most of them were easy targets for anyone lookin' to sneak up on them. A few others he was with are still workin' there, the ones who stay sober.'

Ladigan considered it. Something didn't fit right, but he couldn't figure exactly what it was. Jack Timm liked beating his women, but would he kill them? Why had he tried to kill Prilla? Was the attempt on her simply because of Ladigan's interference or was Prilla hiding something? Whatever the case, it would have to wait until after he found the truth about his brother.

'Why'd you come here, now, Mr Mortimer? Why'd you risk telling me all this?'

The newspaperman stared at the floor for a long moment. When his head came up his eyes were glassy with tears that didn't flow and his voice broke with emotion. 'Earlier today you asked me if I ever lost someone close. Had me a gal at the saloon. She wasn't what most folks would call respectable, but she meant something to me. Might even say I loved her, though I know it wasn't the same for her. She was one of those women killed, after being with Timm, far as I can figure. No one helped her and I don't even know where her body went. Maybe I can help her by helpin' you. Though it won't bring her back, maybe it will afford her a measure of peace.

Least I'm praying it will.'

Ladigan nodded. 'I'm going after that evidence my brother wanted, and Jack Timm.'

'You won't get him to trial in this town, Mr Ladigan. The marshal won't let you take him elsewhere, either.'

'Ain't something you need concern yourself with, Mr Mortimer.' A darkness came into his tone and the newspaperman nodded, face grim.

'Stay here with Prilla. Make sure nothing happens to her or I'll hold you accountable.'

The newspaperman nodded again.

'Least I can do for my girl's memory.'

Ladigan went to the examination room and located the doc's leather satchel, hoping it would have what he needed. He rummaged through it, bringing out a stethoscope and stuffing it in his shirt. He was no safe expert, but could open one given enough time.

He left Prilla and the newspaperman staring after him as he stepped out into the night.

After Ladigan departed, Prilla clutched tighter to the rifle. She watched Mortimer as he angled the big chair towards the door, then settled into it.

'He ain't comin' if he hasn't by now, Mr

Mortimer,' she said, voice steady and confident.

'Jack Timm's a monster, ma'am. Who knows what he might do?'

'He'll run home and lick his wounds. He's a coward at heart.' But a dangerous coward, she amended in her mind. Ladigan was riding into Hell. He didn't know the power of the Timms and there were those two other men with Jack, who'd attacked at the camp. She could sit here like he told her, do nothing the way she always had, take the easy way out. Then if Ladigan didn't return she could keep his horse and belongings and ride out. It was simple enough. Wasn't it?

Help me...

Her mother's scream rose in her mind, startling her, and the newspaperman eyed her with a measure of concern.

'You all right?' he asked.

'No, Mr Mortimer, I ain't. All my life I did what the fine folks in this town do, look out only for myself.'

'Can't really blame them none. They're scared of the Timms. He says the word and they don't eat.'

'That how you feel?'

He nodded. 'I did. I ain't proud of it.'

'Neither am I. Maybe a few days ago it

194

wouldn't have bothered me so much, Mr Mortimer. But Ladigan risked his life to save me. I didn't appreciate it then, called him a damned fool, in fact. But here he goes, risking it again. He's going after Jack Timm for his brother's sake, but also for mine.'

'Reckon you're right about that. He's a strong man. He'll come back. Maybe he'll even do what he says about the Timms.' Something in his voice belied his words.

'But if he don't come back and I just let him get himself killed, nothin's changed. I'm still looking out for just myself, the Timms still own the town and you go back to printing lies about suicidal bar-women in your paper.'

'What are you proposing to do?' Concern now made his voice tremble, concern and fear.

Prilla stood, the rifle resting against the crook of her left arm, determination on her face. She barely had her strength back and everywhere on her hurt like hell, but she refused to let pain sway her decision.

'He bought me a dress, you know that? No man's ever bought me nothin' and not wanted somethin' back for it.'

'I don't understand.' He shook his head.

'No, reckon you wouldn't. Reckon no one

in this town would unless I spelled it out for them. But I ask you, Mr Mortimer, how bad you want things to be different?'

'I ... I can't, Prilla. I'm an old man. I risked enough comin' here tonight.'

'I won't hold it against you, Mr Mortimer. I'm sure Ladigan won't either.' She moved to the door and opened it.

'Now, wait just a minute. Ladigan told us to stay here and told me to protect you.'

She gave him a defiant glare.

'You want to protect me, you'll have to come with me to the Timm place.'

He looked as if he'd suddenly bitten into the wormy end of an apple. He bowed his head and she had her answer.

'I figured as much.' She stepped out into the night, leaving the newspaperman staring after her. She ran down the alley to the back of the livery, legs rubbery but holding up. She would need a horse and the luck of a riverboat gambler, but she would not go back to what was. It was her choice now, and she had made it. Ladigan would not ride into Hell alone.

CHAPTER TEN

Ladigan angled his horse off the trail fifty yards from the outskirts of the Timm mansion. In the distance its moonlight-glazed lines looked eerie and foreboding, silver and shadow melding in menacing contrast.

Reining to a halt, he slipped from the saddle and tethered the horse to an aspen. He swerved right as he scuttled forward, approaching the building, gaze constantly in motion. He scanned the silvered grounds and outbuildings for any sign of movement or threat. Everything was quiet, deathly still.

Lights blazed from within one of the outbuildings and he avoided the dwelling, keeping low. He couldn't chance being spotted by one of Jack Timm's men. They were clumsy, inefficient, but they could sure as hell raise an alarm. They'd also be well within their rights to shoot him on the spot.

Ladigan approached the piazza, skirted left. Only an upper-level room showed any glow. He wondered whether Solomon Timm was even present. He and his wife might have ventured out on another engagement; that would work to Ladigan's advantage. Otherwise he might have had to wait until everyone retired for the night.

What about Jack Timm? Where was he? Here? Ladigan saw no immediate signs the man had crawled back to the mansion after his encounter with Prilla. He might have gone to the saloon, or, worse, he might have decided to take revenge on Prilla immediately. Ladigan had no confidence the newspaperman could protect her but she had a rifle and her fear of Jack Timm would likely make her fast on the trigger.

He paused, unsure whether to go back and make certain she was safe, but decided against it. Jack Timm was a violent man, but he wasn't particularly reckless. He would likely assume she'd run back to the one person who could protect her and bide his time until he could catch her off guard again.

What if you're wrong again, Ladigan? What if it's another mistake?

No, he had to trust his instincts now, let his manhunter's sixth sense serve him the way it always had.

Drawing a deep breath to steel his nerves, Ladigan angled around the mansion, searching for an open window. He discovered more than one and it didn't surprise him: Solomon Timm relied heavily on his hold over the folks of Timmervale keeping away trespassers, along with the armed Gainly and his son's men. The Gild King in his castle.

Ladigan scooted up to a partially opened window and eased it up the rest of the way. Throwing a leg over the sill, he clambered inside. He had selected that particular window because it appeared to give entry into a darkened den. He figured that was the most likely place for a safe and any incriminating evidence that Timm might keep close.

He found a lantern and fished a lucifer from his pocket. He ignited the lamp and kept it turned low. He set it on a mahogany desk. Moonlight arching through the windows helped and his eyes adjusted quickly to the gloom. He pulled the stethoscope from his shirt and set it on the desk. He slid open one of the drawers, rifled through the papers within.

A sound stopped him. Ears pricked, he listened, heart stepping up a beat. He peered at the closed door, holding his breath, but the sound didn't come again and he wasn't entirely sure he'd heard anything at all.

Going back to the drawer contents, he scanned some of the papers, discovering that most were unimportant documents relating to mining concerns. He hadn't figured on Timm's being stupid enough to keep anything incriminating lying in the open, but sometimes men of his stature got full of themselves, made stupid mistakes.

Another sound, just beyond the door, louder. He couldn't move fast enough. The room suddenly blazed with light and a figure stood in the doorway, hand on a switch.

'Gaslighting, Mr Ladigan,' said Cherish Timm, an odd smile playing on her delicate face. 'It's the latest thing.' She brought her other hand from behind her back. Light glinted from a long-bladed knife clutched in her white fingers. Leaning over the desk, he remained motionless as she came into the room, a man stepping in behind her.

'Mr Ladigan, we meet again. This time the round and the match go to me.' Gory scratches showed on Jack Timm's face, caked with blood. His lips and nose were swollen. Ladigan reckoned Jack had Prilla to thank for that. The younger Timm clutched a Winchester.

'You saw me come in?' Ladigan wondered how anyone could have spotted him approaching.

Cherish Timm shook her head.

'The hallway was dark. The lantern glow showed beneath the door, though not by much. My husband was upstairs in his office working, again, leaving me alone the way he does most nights. That old fool, Gainly, retired early. I was just about to tend to Jack's wounds before Solomon discovered Jack's penchant for bargirls turned sour on him again.' She cast Jack a reproving glance.

Ladigan's gaze focused on the knife in her small hand. Something told him the pieces were all here now, but he couldn't yet arrange them in the proper order. The only thing he knew for certain was he'd been caught flatfooted and it would likely be the last mistake he made.

'Your husband hit you, ma'am?' If he had any chance of getting out of this alive, he had to stall, keep Jack Timm off guard. The armed man was the bigger threat of the two. He reckoned he could disarm a lone girl with a knife, but getting to Jack Timm before he pulled the trigger was dubious. Ladigan straightened, slowly stepped around the desk.

'Uh-uh, Mr Ladigan.' Jack Timm levered a shell into the Winchester's chamber. 'No further. I'd hate to make a lot of noise shooting you and bring the old man down here. That wouldn't fit into my plan at all.'

'*Our* plan, Jack dear.' Cherish Timm's voice held a chilled edge. Her gaze centered on Ladigan, a cruelness in her eyes he hadn't seen before. 'As for your question, Mr Ladigan, no, my husband never hits me. Told the old bastard I tripped and fell down the stairs. Fact is, I haven't let the old bastard touch me once since we got hitched. Bad enough I had to let him paw all over me before that.'

Ladigan's brow furrowed.

'I don't understand.'

She let out a cold giggle. 'Jack likes to play rough, Mr Ladigan.'

An uneasy look crossed Jack Timm's mangled features.

'Shut up, Cherish. He don't need to know anything.'

She glared at him. The younger Timm stepped back, and suddenly Ladigan saw who held the reins here. It wasn't Jack Timm, or Solomon. It was Cherish.

The woman ran her fingertips over the knife-blade.

'Don't matter what he knows or where he's going. Least we can satisfy his curiosity.'

Jack's grip tightened on the Winchester.

'The old man might come down.'

'So?' She laughed, a small lethal sound. ''Bout time we make him sign the papers and be done with it anyway. He ain't never going to trust either one of us completely.' She stepped back and eased the door shut, even so.

'Let's just get rid of him.'

'Jack, Jack, so impatient. I gave you a bit of time to play with him but you didn't do a very good job of it, did you? Otherwise he wouldn't be here now. Perhaps the fine people of Timmervale aren't as in your pocket as you thought.'

'Who are you, Mrs. Timm?' Ladigan edged a step closer, stopping as Jack motioned with the rifle. The distance was still too far. He couldn't reach the man before a bullet found him.

'I'm Mrs. Solomon Timm, my dear man. A poor hurdy-gurdy gal rescued from the clutches of sin by an old man whose wife had passed on, poor thing.'

'Cherish, that's my ma you're talkin' about. Don't keep tellin'—'

She flashed the knife around and sliced a clean cut across his shoulder. It separated his shirt fabric and bled, but wasn't deep.

'Be a good little boy, Jack, and shut the hell up.'

Jack Timm gritted his teeth, anger blazing his eyes, but his rifle didn't waver.

'You see, when Solomon Timm married me, Mr Ladigan, he wasn't quite as stupid as I hoped. There's still the matter of changing the will and certain papers that would leave this all to me and Jack.' Her gaze raked Ladigan, smile growing colder. 'He looks like his brother, doesn't he, Jack? Right handsome fella in his own way. Maybe if things weren't the way they are...'

'You saw my brother?' The dark suspicion in his gut exploded. The answer was right before him now and he knew he would not find his kin alive. It was over, the hammer had fallen.

'Caught him in much the same position as you, Mr Ladigan ... John, may I call you John?' She giggled, the sound somehow dark and insane. ''Course I can. He had the safe half open, you know. Had near everything he needed before I snuck up on him and put a knife in his slats.'

The news crashed into him like a blow and Ladigan near staggered under it.

'You killed him...'

'No, she didn't.' Jack Timm uttered a chopped laugh. 'She stabbed him. He was still alive when I buried him. Don't worry though, he's got plenty of company, what with those whores and the doc lying there next to him.'

'You're a dead man, Timm.' Ladigan said it low and final. His search was over His brother was dead and these two were responsible. A numbed shock gripped him. He readied himself for a lunge at Jack Timm, though it was certain suicide.

'You're in no position to promise anything, Mr Lad – *John*,' said Cherish, but Jack Timm took a step backward and his hands bleached as he gripped the rifle tighter.

Ladigan's gaze didn't waver from the younger Timm.

'Would you like to know what your brother discovered?' she continued. 'I'm sure who-ever set you on us couldn't have known the details. I hope you'll tell me who it was so we can thank him – or is it her? – properly.'

His gaze shifted to her. Muscles knotted and quivered to either side of his jaw.

'You were raped. There was a child. Your husband didn't want the scandal.'

She raised an eyebrow.

'Well, well, I would have thought no one had even learned that much, but you're only half-right. I was never raped but yes I carried a child and yes, my husband didn't want the

205

scandal. Can't have the Timm name sullied. Since I wanted to get my hands on his holdings I saw the wisdom of his words.'

'If you weren't raped who–'

She laughed, cutting him off.

'Like I said, Jack likes to play rough.'

Ladigan's gaze went back to Jack Timm, who had a hard time keeping still.

'You were the father?'

He nodded. 'I love Cherish. She's my age anyhow and we're going to have all this soon.' He ducked his chin at the room. 'We told the old man she was raped. He would have killed me with his bare hands if he had discovered I was with her.'

The pieces locked together in a perfect fit. Jack Timm and Cherish had covered up the birth of a child, not only protecting the Timm name, but their own greedy plans. Solomon Timm accepted his wife's explanation, likely after one of Jack's rough sessions with her made the rape story look all too realistic. Tom had discovered some or most of the story somehow, learned about the child. But while looking for back-up evidence he had stumbled into more than he thought. Cherish and Jack had caught him, the way they caught Ladigan tonight. He saw one missing piece, however.

'Those saloon girls in town...?' Ladigan's gaze stayed locked with Jack Timm's.

Cherish Timm's face hardened, her beauty dropping away as if she'd removed a mask.

'Jack's insatiable, I think. I've told him he best stay away from those girls but he don't listen clearly sometimes. I'm right possessive, you might say. I clean up his messes, least the ones I was able to catch drunk or passed out. I'd get to the rest sooner or later, especially that favorite of his – what was her name, Jack dear? Oh, yes, Prilla, I reckon it was.'

Jack flinched as if hit. It was clear he had thought he kept that one a secret from her.

Ladigan used the distraction to slide forward a few more inches, but it wasn't enough.

'That all you want to know, now, John?' Her cold smile returned. 'Reckon it's time you joined your brother, then, don't you think? You're going to turn around and put your hands flat on the desk, unless you want Jack to shoot you where you stand. I promise it'll be quick.'

She intended to put the knife in his back if he complied. If he didn't, they would risk the noise and put lead in him. That left him one option, a long-shot: If he could somehow let her get close enough to grab and use as a shield...

A shot crashed out, the sound like thunder in the room.

Jack Timm jumped, letting out a girlish screech and dropping his rifle, which by some quirk failed to discharge. He grabbed at his ear, blood running between his fingers. 'Christamighty, my ear, someone shot off my goddamn ear!'

'I was aiming between your eyes, you vicious sonofabitch!' Prilla's voice came from the window through which Ladigan had entered. She was perched half-over the sill, a Winchester in her hands still aimed at Jack Timm.

Cherish lunged, swinging the knife in a short arc. The move caught Ladigan off guard. He got an arm up to protect his face but the blade tore through his shirt sleeve and sliced a shallow gash across his forearm.

Cherish Timm swung the knife again in a backhanded sweep. He twisted away, the blade nearly cleaving off the tip of his nose.

He snapped a short right that cracked against the woman's jaw. Her eyes went wide. She stumbled backwards, crashing to the floor on her rump. She gazed forward, a dazed look in her eyes, but still held the knife.

Jack Timm danced about, cursing and bleeding. Prilla kept the rifle leveled on him from the window.

The room door burst open and Solomon Timm, brought by the gunfire, stood on the threshold, a Smith & Wesson in his hand.

'What the hell is the meaning of this?' His voice came startled, but commanding. He was a man used to walking into tough situations, taking control, but he apparently wasn't prepared for what he found. His gaze jumped from Ladigan to Jack to Cherish, whose eyes had cleared and who was staring at Ladigan with spite.

'Cherish...' Solomon Timm's voice dropped to a whisper.

'You disgusting old man!' Her gaze shifted to the elder Timm. 'You make me sick. You with your sour breath and lard belly. You should have given me what's mine. I deserve it for marryin' the likes of you!'

Solomon Timm's face dropped, and a wounded look came into his eyes. He glanced at his son, who had calmed but was still holding his bleeding ear, piecing together what was happening, at least enough of it to realize his marriage had been a lie.

Cherish Timm let out a screech and grabbed for the rifle on the floor. She got her hands around it and came to her feet faster than Ladigan would have thought possible.

She swung up the Winchester. Ladigan's hand swept for his Peacemaker.

Instinct took over, guiding his aim. The Colt thundered.

Cherish Timm jerked, looked down at the red rose blossoming on the front of her yellow dress, just over her heart.

'J-Jack...' Her voice came weak, pleading. She dropped, crumpling into a heap. The Winchester fired as it hit the floor; the bullet buried itself in a wall.

'No...' Solomon Timm shook his head and lowered his gun. He went to her, knelt, cradling her head on his lap.

She looked up at him with glazed eyes, blood snaking from the corner of her mouth.

'Silly old bastard...' she whispered. Then her head lolled back and her eyes stared sightlessly at the ceiling.

Jack Timm appeared to be ready to lunge for the old man's Smith & Wesson but Ladigan shifted his aim and he froze.

'I'm takin' your son, Timm,' Ladigan said to Solomon, a broken man who was poised over his wife's body, tears running down his face. 'He's responsible for that baby you sent away and for my brother's death, as well as nearly killing a friend of mine. He'll hang for his crimes.'

The older man looked at his son with disgust and fury, but worse, blame, blame for ruining all he had known and for destroying the Timm name.

'Take him.' He turned his attention back to his wife.

Two men appeared in the doorway, Burgis and Linch, both holding guns that leveled on Ladigan.

Jack Timm smiled suddenly.

'Kill him!' he ordered. Both men hesitated, peering at the old man on the floor, then at the manhunter.

Ladigan's voice came steady and promising.

'You got yourselves a choice, boys. You can kill me and let Jack keep on the way he has until the law comes for him and hangs you as accessories to murder, or you can step away and let me take him for hanging.'

The men glanced at Jack, then at each other. They holstered their weapons and walked off.

Ladigan motioned with his Peacemaker and forced Jack Timm to walk ahead of him. He paused at the door, looked down at

Solomon Timm.

'What was the child, Mr Timm?'

He looked up, bleary-eyed.

'Huh? Oh ... she ... a little girl. She's about two now. I send money...'

'Bet that makes you feel better...' Ladigan frowned, then motioned Jack Timm forward again.

They went out into the night, Jack sweating suddenly, eyes darting. Prilla had a horse from the livery at the far end of the property and fetched it, leading it by the reins as she walked beside them. When they reached the spot where Ladigan had tethered his own mount, she held the Winchester on the prisoner while Ladigan wrapped the man's wrists with the saddle rope, then tied it to the saddle. He mounted, eye on Jack Timm, while Prilla climbed aboard her own horse. They started towards Timmervale, the younger Timm walking behind, led by the wrists.

Half-way to town Jack Timm seemed either to get his confidence back or go plumb loco. Ladigan never was quite sure which.

'No one will find me guilty in Timmervale, Ladigan. I'll get off. Then I'm gonna come back and kill you for takin' Cherish from me. Gonna kill your no-good whore, too.

You hear me, Ladigan?' He let out a high-pitched laugh and spat in defiance.

Ladigan tensed, knowing things would change once the story of Jack and Cherish hit the papers, but also not deluding himself: Jack Timm might have enough friends left thinking they could get a handout for aiding him. He could chance the man coming after him, but wouldn't risk him coming after Prilla.

'I hear you, Jack...' Ladigan reined up. 'I hear you.'

As Ladigan dismounted, Jack Timm's face lost its defiance. Prilla reined up beside them, confusion on her face.

Ladigan plucked the Bowie knife from his bootsheath and sliced the connecting rope from Jack Timm, leaving only the man's wrists tightly tied. He glanced at Prilla. 'Keep your rifle on him. Shoot him if he so much as sneezes.' She nodded.

He began fashioning a makeshift noose from the length of rope. When he'd got it the way he wanted, he went to a tree beside the trail, one with a sturdy branch just high enough off the ground.

Prilla kept her Winchester trained on Jack Timm, whose eyes widened.

'What the hell are you doing?' Timm's

voice came out half a scream, half a plea.

Ladigan looked at him, features dark.

'You convinced me, Jack. You convinced me I'd never get conviction in Timmervale, so I'm gonna sidestep the trial and pronounce sentence right now. You buried my brother alive. You beat the hell out of that girl right there.' He nudged his head at Prilla. 'Reckon I don't give a damn if you come after me. I got nothing left, now. But I won't let you hurt Prilla or anyone else ever again.'

'Jesus, Ladigan, you can't just hang me.' Fear danced in Jack Timm's eyes.

'Get up on the horse.'

'The hell I will!' Jack Timm stood defiant but trembling.

Ladigan drew his Peacemaker.

'You can do it under your own power or I'll shoot out your kneecaps and hoist you up there myself.'

Fear turned to panic on Jack Timm's face. He went to the bay and stuck a foot in the stirrup. Ladigan shoved him up into the saddle, then led the mount to the tree, just beneath the noose.

'Prilla, put it around his neck.' She looked at Ladigan with a puzzled expression, then thrust her rifle into its saddleboot. Guiding her horse over to the bay, she reached out and grasped the noose.

'Prilla, you can't do this. You have to help me, please, this is murder.'

She stared into his terror-stained eyes.

'Way you helped me? Way you let the town help me?' She placed the noose over his neck and jerked it tight. 'Goodbye, Jack.'

'Noooo!' Jack Timm screamed.

She looked at him again, swallowed hard and turned away, pity in her eyes, but resolution also.

'Go back to town,' Ladigan said, looking at her. She nodded, glancing one last time at Jack Timm, then at Ladigan, before heeling her horse into a fast gait towards Timmervale.

Jack Timm wouldn't go quick and he wanted to spare her that. Watching a man die wasn't pretty.

Saying a small prayer for his brother, Ladigan grasped his bay's reins and led the horse from beneath Jack Timm.

Ladigan walked back into town, the body of Jack Timm draped over the bay's saddle. Marshal Pierson stepped out onto the boardwalk, glanced at the body and froze.

'Christ, Ladigan, what you gone and done?'

Ladigan looked at him and kept all expression off his face.

'I punished a man for his crimes, Marshal. The story will come out soon enough. You plan on arresting me?'

The marshal peered at him, knowing he would never take this man in, then turned and headed back into his office. He was free of Jack Timm's influence, but he would need to find a way to live with himself.

A man came down the boardwalk, steps slow and deliberate, a grim expression on his face.

Ladigan pulled the body from his horse and laid it on the boardwalk.

'Mr Mortimer, reckon you know who the funeral man is in this town?'

The newspaperman nodded.

'I'll take care of it. What happened?'

Ladigan explained the events at the Timm mansion and Jack's hanging.

'Thank you, Mr Ladigan.' Mortimer glanced at the body, frowning but looking relieved at the same time. 'Thank you for freeing this town and for Eva's memory.'

'Eva?'

'She's the gal I told you about.'

Ladigan nodded. The sorrow inside him burned, made his soul feel heavy. Tom was gone and he had known it all along, no matter how hard he had struggled to deny it. He knew why he had made mistakes and why he had questioned his cause: he had simply been grieving deep inside, wherever grief lived since the day his parents died. He just hadn't recognized or admitted it. Now all that grief was surging up and taking hold of him. He reckoned he didn't know what the hell he would do with himself now that he had nothing.

'She's got peace now.' Mortimer's voice brought him from his dark thoughts.

Peace. Ladigan reckoned that wasn't what he had but justice would have to do.

'I reckon she does, Mr Mortimer. Along with those other gals Cherish killed. Just see to it your paper prints the truth.'

'I owe you that much, Mr Ladigan.'

'Reckon it's my brother who's owed. It was his story.'

'I'll see to it everyone knows it, too.'

'Be obliged. I'd appreciate it if you saw to my brother getting a proper burial. We had no other kin.'

Mortimer nodded.

'Consider it done, sir. You don't want to be here?'

'No.' He swallowed hard, preferring to

recollect Tom as he was in the tintype, smiling, full of life. 'No.'

He led his horse towards the livery.

Bright sunlight stung his eyes and he reckoned he hadn't even lasted a minute after settling into the chair in the back room of the sawbones' office. Prilla was already asleep by the time he got back, exhausted from her ordeal.

The bright day brought little peace to John Ladigan and little sense of accomplishment. He had found his brother and brought down his killers. It should have felt better, but it didn't. It felt ... *empty*, and he felt alone.

That feeling was made worse by the fact she was gone when he woke. The bed was empty but his gear was all still here.

He forced himself out of the chair and strapped on his gunbelt. Collecting the rifle – Prilla had taken one of those – he went to the livery. His big bay still resided in the stall, but the attendant was worked up into a lather.

'She stole one of my horses! Held me at gunpoint, even.'

Ladigan pulled the roll of greenbacks from his pocket and doled out far more than the horse was worth.

'She borrowed it.'

The man's eyes widened and he nodded to himself.

'She borrowed it,' he repeated, walking away.

Ladigan saddled his horse and left Timmervale behind him, a place of corruption and death, of lost hope and the false happiness money could buy. Change would come, he reckoned, brought about by the fall of Timmervale's first family, but likely the folks would go on much the same. Least, too many of them. Maybe he was too cynical.

He made one stop, buying a morning paper and reading the lead article that told all about the fall of the Timms. The article carried his brother's byline and he almost smiled.

It didn't take him long to catch up to Prilla.

He found her horse tied to a tree and her at trailside, leaning over, throwing up again. She wore the gingham dress he'd bought for her. Guiding his horse towards her, he looked down as she shakily came to her feet.

'More often than not I find you in that position,' he said, no humor in his voice. She didn't answer and went for her horse, untying him and mounting.

She led it back onto the trail and rode

beside him, silent for a while.

'Why'd you run off again?' he asked after near ten minutes passed, not sure he wanted to know the answer.

'I was scared.' Her voice came low, trembly.

'Scared? Timm's dead. He won't hurt you again.'

'I was scared of you, what I've been startin' to feel for you.'

He looked straight ahead, sighed.

'So you run?'

'You're not a fool, like I said, Ladigan. You're a kind man, a special man. You're a man who wouldn't want to be with a woman like me.'

'What type of woman is that, Prilla? A woman who decided to help me when I told her to stay put and save herself? Timm would have won if not for you.'

'You know what I am, Ladigan.'

'I know what you used to be.'

She peered at him, face serious.

'You want to know what Timm asked me to do that night he almost cut my ear off?'

He shrugged. 'If you want to tell me.'

Her gaze shifted straight ahead.

'I ain't sick because he beat me. I'm sick because he made me with child. That night he told me I had to get rid of it, that he would have someone cut it out of me and no one would ever know. Then I could go back to being his favorite, no one the wiser.'

'You said no, I take it.'

'Damn right I said no. Other girls, they would have done anything to be on his good side. He was brutal but he wasn't cheap. But my ma tried to raise me before ... before she was killed. I plan to do the same for my child, even if it was from a bastard like Timm.'

'How you plan on livin'? Where you plan on goin'?'

She shrugged, pale and trembling, but somehow looking more dignified.

'I don't know.'

'How about St Louis?'

'St Louis?'

'There's a little girl there without a family, in a foundling home.'

She peered at him, shock on her face, but joy leaping into her eyes.

'Why? Why would you take a child who came from the Timms, from someone who killed...?' She went silent a moment. 'I'm sorry...'

'From someone who killed my brother? It's all right to say it. I denied it myself for too long. But if you knew Tom you'd know this is what he would want. Ain't that little girl's fault what happened. I'm alone now and I'm tired of manhunting. Took me some time to figure it out but I figure her and I could be alone together. I got enough money and I reckon a business back East might be a welcome change of pace.' He paused. 'I also reckon she could use a brother or sister.' He gazed at her and saw a tear slip from her eye.

'St Louis's a long ways,' she said, emotion choking her voice. 'I'm gonna have to pee a thousand times.'

'You and the horses...' He smiled.

'Maybe I love you, Ladigan.' It was almost inaudible.

'Maybe I love you, too.'

The publishers hope that this book has given you enjoyable reading. Large Print Books are especially designed to be as easy to see and hold as possible. If you wish a complete list of our books please ask at your local library or write directly to:

Dales Large Print Books
Magna House, Long Preston,
Skipton, North Yorkshire.
BD23 4ND

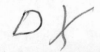